Once Upon a Phone

Larry Enright

Once Upon a Phone

© 2024 Larry Enright

Published by Lawrence P. Enright

Visit the author's website:
http://www.larryenright.com

For the child in all of us

Once Upon a Phone was first published as a twenty-eight-episode serial. Hence, the episode titles, numbers, and original notes from the author intended to keep you reading. If you've already read the story as a serial, you may be bored with this book because it's a compilation of the twenty-eight episodes you already read. The illustrations are new.

1) Amelia Needs a Phone

Her full name was Amelia Rose Gardiner, but she never used Rose because her initials would have spelled ARG. Her first name came from a grandmother she only knew from an old photo, and her middle name came from a relative she didn't know at all. Her last name, of course, came from Mom and Dad. They had actual first names. Mom's was Martha, and Dad's was Bernard, but no one ever called them that around the house, including them. It was too confusing.

Amelia was slender like Mom and had her red hair and freckles. She was 4'2" by the marks on the doorjamb that Grandma Jane made when Dad was growing up and fifty-five pounds on the bathroom scale when she checked that morning, which she did every morning.

Amelia lived with Mom and Dad, her four siblings, and Grandpa Ralph at 6 Brook Lane, just north of the cutoff on Business Route 5. It was Grandpa Ralph's house and overlooked the Hook Inlet and the village of Hook by the Sea. The oldest of the five children was twenty-year-old Bobby, named for Mom's father. Next was Junior. He was nineteen and got his name from Dad. He wasn't a junior. He didn't have the same middle name. That's just what everyone called him. Next was eighteen-year-old Ralphy, who got his name from Grandpa Ralph, and then seventeen-year-old Ruth, not named after anyone. Her superpower was annoying people. Finally came Amelia, who was exactly ten years and 157 days old.

In contrast, Hook by the Sea, population 3,307, was significantly older. Thanks to Ruth, a much younger and more naïve Amelia once believed that the village was named for Captain Hook. The town just up the coast was supposedly called Panville, where Peter and his lost boys had their hideout, and lovely Wendy Darling was living next door in Mayor Peterman's attic. It took Grandma Jane to convince her that Hook was actually named for the fishhook shape of the inlet, that Lambert was the name of the next town up the coast, and that the Wendy next door was the Peterman's youngest daughter, who liked to play in the attic with her friends. Contrary to Ruth, the people who first settled the area weren't lost boys being chased by pirates. They were ordinary people who settled in an isolated lobster-rich inlet 312 years ago and became lobstermen and then fishermen when the lobsters ran out.

The Gardiners had been fishermen, at least as far back as Great Grandpa Joseph. Beyond that, the details were sketchy. There could have been a pirate or two in the family, and there might have been a horse thief on Grandma Jane's side, but that page of the family Bible was conveniently missing, and Grandpa Ralph claimed his memory wasn't what it used to be. Their boat, the Lady Jane, was a twenty-five-foot trawler. Like the Gardiners' house, it belonged to Grandpa Ralph. He named it for Grandma Jane, who died when Amelia was seven. That was when Dad took over and Grandpa Ralph retired.

Everyone had their part in the family business. Dad was Captain of the Jane. Amelia's brothers Bobby and Junior were its full-time crew, each having entered the family business at sixteen, intending to make a career of it, and Ralphy, who was going to college to become a marine biologist and helped out when he was home on breaks. Grandpa Ralph kept the books and told other people what to do. It *was* still his boat, though he never set foot on it after Grandma Jane died. Mom's job was getting up at 4:30 a.m. every day except Sunday to make breakfast, pack lunches, and see the men off in time for the sunrise catch. That left Ruth, who had nothing to do with fishing unless you count being volunteered by Mom to make fish sandwiches for the church bazaar every year, and Amelia.

Amelia's contribution was doing chores. She trimmed. She raked. She was in charge of mowing the front yard after Grandpa Ralph decided he'd had enough of Mr. Peterman's complaining about it. On cleaning day, her job was dusting unless Ruth had conveniently disappeared again. Then, it was dusting *and* vacuuming. She set the table, cleared it, and did the dishes—often when it was someone else's turn. She was Mom's menu consultant and sous-chef. She took out the garbage and turned the compost pile every day. She did everything asked of her because she liked helping, and she did it all pro bono.

The fact that Amelia didn't even have enough money saved to open a bank account and had no source of income other than the birthday and Christmas cards her godparents sent every year didn't matter until she was almost nine. That was when she asked for a phone, ostensibly for school, and the answer was no. Her parents said it didn't matter that 73.2% of her class and 93.4% of the ones homeschooling like her had one. It was two years of $55.65 a month until the phone was paid off and $15.00 a month plus tax thereafter, and they simply couldn't afford it.

Undeterred and firmly believing that birthdays

were exceptions to every rule regarding how much Mom and Dad could afford, Amelia asked for a phone for her ninth birthday and again on her tenth. She offered to have it count for three birthdays and two Christmases. She even told them they'd never have to give her another gift again for the rest of her life, but the answer was always no. And they wouldn't even consider an allowance for extra chores instead of the big fat nothing she was currently getting, or as Dad put it, her room and board, her clothing, her education, and her laptop.

Not one to give up so easily, Amelia went shopping for a better answer from Grandpa Ralph but found neither moral support nor a secondary source of funding, only advice—if you need money, get a job. She'd listened to Grandpa Ralph's advice over the years, more so during the last three that he'd been home instead of out on the ocean fishing. Sometimes, she took it. Sometimes she didn't.

This time, she did, beginning with a brief foray into babysitting, canvassing her neighbors on Brook Lane. Unfortunately, their children were either too old for her, she was too young for them, or they were just a handful, or whatever. The reasons all amounted to the same—Come back when you're older.

At Grandpa Ralph's suggestion, she called the County Gazette to see if she could get a paper route. He read the newspaper every day, and someone had to deliver it. It didn't just magically appear in the bushes out front every afternoon. Unfortunately, the Gazette didn't need any paperboys. Some guy with a van did the whole village. Before thanking them for their time and saying goodbye, Amelia told them that Grandpa Ralph would appreciate it if the guy with the van could work on his aim.

Amelia next considered becoming a venture capitalist and parlaying her savings into a fortune big enough to buy a phone and who knows what else. That involved a visit to the piggy bank. Hers was one of Grandpa Ralph's old cigar boxes. He liked to smoke them coming home on a quiet sea after a long day trawling, or as Grandma Jane used to say, he smoked them anytime, anywhere, and it was disgusting. The box Amelia kept in her top drawer was the last one he'd bought before turning over the Jane to Dad. He quit a lot of things after Grandma Jane died. Inside the box, along with a few odds and ends worth hiding in an underwear drawer, was Amelia's life savings— twenty-three dollars and change. By her calculations, if she opened a savings account, she would have almost enough to buy that cute case she wanted for the phone that would be obsolete by the time she could afford it.

Next, relying on her proven yard skills and Grandpa Ralph's borrowed tools, Amelia started a lawn-care service. Step one was getting the word out, so she printed flyers and stuffed one in every mailbox on Brook Lane. Step two was going door to door to see who was interested, starting with the Peterman's. Mayor Peterman was happy to oblige and gave her a dollar to rake his yard, which took Amelia an hour and a half until he was satisfied no more leaves would be falling that afternoon. At sixty-seven cents an hour (rounded up), she decided she could make more looking for change on the sidewalk.

Giving up on self-employment, she tried to find work in the village, but the 24-hour Stop-N-Shop at the light on Business 5, Clara's Gift Shop, Bower's Pharmacy, and everywhere else she asked all told her she had to be fourteen before she could work legally. Although no job was to be found that day, the effort wasn't a total waste. She found a quarter and three pennies on the sidewalk.

Out of ideas, she went to the library. Before the Internet, that was where everyone went to get answers to their questions. She and Mom shelved books there on Thursdays and were friends with Clara Finnerty, the librarian, who suggested that Amelia try Granger's Market over on Main. Her nephew, Ricky, was fourteen and had been working there as a delivery boy since he was eleven. Though his pay was in tips only, he was always telling her how much he made. Last she heard, he was saving up for a new bike.

That sounded promising. Mom could have gone up the coast to the supermarket in Lambert to shop for groceries. Most of her friends did. It wasn't that far, and they were always telling her how the prices were cheaper and the selection better there, but Mom always shopped at Granger's because she and Mrs. Granger were friends. And Dad could have sold his catch to anyone, but he always gave Granger's first crack at it.

That was the deal Don and Grandpa Ralph had struck and sealed with a handshake back when the Jane was his to captain. And Amelia knew the Grangers from the market and church well enough to say hello and goodbye. That had to count for something. Given that the worst Mr. Granger could say was what everyone else had, she asked.

As luck would have it, Don Granger was indeed looking for someone. One of his delivery boys quit, and he needed one more to fill out the crew. Unfortunately, ten was too young, Amelia was a girl, and the job was for a delivery boy, as it said on their Granger T-shirts.

According to some, Amelia was precocious. Ask Grandpa Ralph, and she was too big for her britches. In either case, Amelia pointed out that denying a person a job based on their age or gender was discrimination. She also pointed out that Mom was homeschooling her because she was smart like her. Of course, she explained, that wasn't the reason for homeschooling at first. The pandemic was why she started, but it was during lockdown she realized going to school was more like watching Sunday afternoon football with Grandpa Ralph. It took three hours to watch a one-hour contest in which only eighteen minutes on average was actual playing time. School was just as boring, and she could go faster if only they'd let her. So she asked, they did, and she never looked back. She was already in the seventh grade despite only being ten. She'd started seventh at the beginning of the summer, and Mom thought she could finish by Christmas if she would ever complete her stupid science project. She was smart and reliable, could make change without a calculator, and besides, he hired Ricky when he was eleven, and she'd been ten for 157 days, which meant she was forty-three percent of the way there. Her credentials were impressive, and her points were all well made, but it took a call to Mom and some humiliating begging and pleading before Amelia was officially a Granger's Market delivery boy.

After their handshake to seal the deal, Don read her the fine print. His boys were expected to work at least two weekdays after school until closing at 6:00 p.m. and six hours on Saturdays. Her assigned weekdays were Tuesday and Wednesday, but she could come every day they were open if she wanted. It was up to her. The job paid tips only, meaning he wasn't paying her to sit around doing nothing. In fact, he wasn't paying her at all. It was the customers who paid her, and the customers only tipped what they thought was fair. The harder she worked, the better she'd do. The better she did, the better they'd tip. The better they tipped, the sooner she'd get her phone.

Note from the Author

Amelia Gardiner is a fictional character. So are Grandpa Ralph, Mom, Dad, Bobby, Junior, Ralphy, and even Ruth the Annoying. Everything that happens to them is fictional. Any resemblance to you is not on purpose. That was your disclaimer.

As I write this, forty-two percent of ten-year-olds in the U.S. have a cell phone. Nearly seventy percent have one by age twelve. Over ninety percent of adults have one. Unfortunately, Mom, Dad, and Grandpa Ralph are among the ten percent who don't, and therein lies the problem for our young heroine. But, as Grandpa Ralph once said, that girl's a handful in a hurry, so if you're interested in seeing where this all leads, read on. Otherwise, thanks for coming this far. I hope it didn't hurt too much.

2) Granger's Market

The village of Hook by the Sea occupied 3.1 square miles of coastline, starting at the Hook Point Lighthouse and continuing around the inlet to the Northside Docks on the opposite side. The western cliffs ringing the inlet made the village longer than it was wide and shaped more or less like a banana. Hook had a local government, a post office with its own ZIP code, a public library, and a welcome center in Room 115 of the municipal building. It had a police department, a volunteer fire department, a municipal water company, and three automated trash trucks that picked up trash one week and recycling the next. There was one gas station that came with the Stop-N-Shop at the light on Business 5 and one bank with a drive-thru window and ATM. There was a pharmacy that filled prescriptions half now and the rest when it came in, and a hardware store where some of the merchandise dated to the fifties.

Hook had one grocery store, Granger's Market, at the corner of Broad and Main in downtown Hook. It was open Monday through Saturday, and parking was free in the church lot across Broad unless you left your shopping cart there instead of returning it to the store to get your quarter deposit back. Then it cost you a quarter, which Granger's donated to the church. Don and Abigail Granger were second-generation market owners, having inherited the business from Don's father, Cornelius, who used his GI Bill money after World War II to buy Sutter's, the grocery store he'd grown up with that was going out of business. Always pleasant and ever-smiling, Abigail ran the retail end of things. She was the face of the company, the greeter at the door, the one who got fetched when you asked to see the manager. Don, whose skills lay elsewhere, took care of the books, ordering, shipping, and receiving. He was the boss of everything behind the "Employees Only" sign. The Grangers had two teenage boys, Todd and Toby, who helped out after school and on weekends, and there were a few part-timers who'd been with them on and off for years, but it was Don and Abigail who spent the long hours and many nights keeping the lights on.

The church across Broad St. benefiting from its decision to allow Granger's customers to park in their lot was the Church of St. Peter. The diocese built St. Pete's on the former site of the Church of St. Andrew, which burned to the ground. In the Bible, Andrew and Peter were brothers. They were the first apostles and the first fishers of men. Which of them should, therefore, be the patron saint of fishermen was and still is a point of contention among scholars. Hook chose Andrew when they were lobstermen. Lobsters are crustaceans, not fish. His church burnt down. The diocese didn't switch them over to St. Peter because he made Pope, and they should have known better. Hook was a bona fide fishing village by then. They wanted a bigger and better St. Andrew's for North Hook, a growing community needing more churches and Catholic K through 12 schools, so they built a much smaller St. Peter's in its place in the village. They kept the old rectory — that had been far enough away from the fire. The convent and grade school were closer and not so lucky. Those became the parking lot only used for Mass on Sundays and shopping at Granger's every other day.

The majestic Hotel Hook stood catty-corner from Granger's. As indicated by the sign on its front door directing inquiries to Room 115 of the municipal building, the three-story historic site no longer operated as a hotel. It was only open from Memorial Day through Labor Day. Across from that was Wilson's Hardware, circa 1949, built on the site of a general store. Wilson's was where people went to ask for advice on all things DIY and catch up on the latest news. Fifty years ago, they sold penny candy. Now, there's an ATM outside if you're short on cash. Bower's Pharmacy, Clara's Gifts, the post office, the library, and the municipal building were all within a block of Granger's.

Granger's was more than just a grocery store. It was an institution in Hook not only because it had most of what you'd expect from a supermarket without having to drive to Lambert but also because it was the only place you could find Lester's Homemade Halibut Jerky and Greta's Famous Jam and fresh fish delivered daily by boats like the Lady Jane. Granger's did what they could to help local businesses and always had at least one good cause they supported with coin boxes and signs. Abigail volunteered at the food bank on Tuesday mornings and often donated groceries Granger's couldn't sell but could give away. Don managed a little league team when the kids were off school for the summer. He even paid for their Granger Pirates uniforms. The Grangers supported the community, and the community supported them by shopping there at slightly higher prices and trying not to complain too much, especially around Don.

Don Granger considered himself a frugal man. Grandpa Ralph called him a cheapskate, which is how he got tricked into that handshake deal that gave Don the first crack at everything. "Frugal" was why Don still didn't have a ceiling over his office in the back, why he had no full-time employees with employee benefits, and why Granger's offered free delivery.

The idea came to him one day while attending a Rotary meeting at the Lambert Country Club. Don was not himself a golfer, but some of his Rotary friends were, and he enjoyed hobnobbing with them. One was boring him with a stroke-by-stroke account of his latest golf round when Don realized something. Golfers hired caddies, most of them were teenagers, and country clubs like Lambert didn't pay them to sit around all day waiting for a job that might never come. They didn't pay them at all. The caddies weren't employees of the club. The golfers employed them and paid them to carry thirty pounds of equipment on a three-and-a-half mile hike, find their stray balls, and cheat on their scorecards. What the golfers tipped was entirely up to them. The club merely provided the caddies a place to sit around and do nothing on their own time, hoping for a gig to make it worthwhile.

Don thought the model was perfect for what he had in mind, so perfect he called it Granger's Special Delivery. He marketed it as a free service and convinced four teenagers hanging around the caddy shack to give the delivery boy business a shot. As it turned out, caddying was where the real money was, and Don ended up relying on a demographic with much lower expectations—kids too young to get a real job but old enough to carry a shopping bag, kids desperate for a phone like Amelia.

Note from the Author

Kids can be babysitters, papergirls, cookie-sellers, pet-sitters, survey-takers, dog walkers, golf caddies, errand runners, lemonade stand owners, leaf rakers, lawn mowers, hedge trimmers, weed pullers, and delivery persons, especially when it involves money. One summer between high school years, I was a golf caddy for precisely one day. I got to carry exactly one bag for exactly one round. I don't remember my tip, but it wasn't enough to cover what I'd spent on snacks waiting around all day with the other kids. I also remember how hard it was lugging that stupid bag around for all 104 of my golfer's shots, and I don't recall how many balls were lost, but it wasn't zero. I'm afraid I wasn't a good caddy, but Amelia will fare better at Granger's. She'll attend her first standup meeting when we next see her.

3) Stand-up Meeting

Amelia knew approximately how long it took to walk from her house, down Brook Lane to Business 5, up Business 5, and down Main to Granger's. However, she timed it the day before anyway and arrived precisely as planned on Saturday morning. She was wearing her favorite cargo pants, pink tennis shoes, and one of Ruth's tops she'd borrowed without asking because her favorite was in the hamper under her brother's smelly jeans, and Ruth was nowhere to be found, as usual. A metallic-blue phone peeked out of her side pocket, not too obvious, just enough to look cool. Her brother Ralphy was home from school for the weekend and was out on the Jane with Dad, Bobby, and Junior. He'd loaned it to her for the day because he couldn't get cell reception that far offshore anyway, and Mom made him.

Like many fall mornings on the inlet, it was breezy and cool. Forecasters were calling for gradual warming throughout the day as the prevailing winds carried the clouds out to sea. Grandpa Ralph's knees said otherwise. It was going to rain, and she'd be a fool not to wear a raincoat or at least take an umbrella. Amelia didn't do either. Grandpa Ralph's arthritis didn't predict the weather. Computer models did.

Saturday was Granger's busiest day. Mom shopped there on Wednesdays for that reason. This Saturday was no exception. Even the self-checkout had a line, and no one ever used that because no one was ever around to help when things went wrong, which they always did. When Amelia went inside, Mrs. Granger was with a customer explaining why they were not getting a discount even though they were doing the cashier's job. Amelia was a welcome interruption. After determining that their families were both fine and the weather was always unpredictable in Hook that time of year, Abigail presented Granger's newest independent contractor (should anyone from the IRS ask) with a green Granger Market baseball cap and matching Granger T on which she'd stitched "Delivery Boy."

She had her son Toby show Amelia to the conference room, which turned out to be through the "Employees Only" door, past the storeroom, and out back under the awning in the alley beside the dumpsters. Don was waiting there with the crew she was supposed to fill out: the Jolly Green Giant, the Lucky Charms leprechaun, and Ricky Finnerty. Ricky kept his hair short, and the sleeves of his Granger T rolled up tight so you knew what you were messing with should you get in his way. That pack of cigarettes he was hiding in his shirt pocket dared anyone to say something about him being underage. Amelia was 4' 2" and stuck forever at fifty-five pounds. Ricky was a foot taller and pushing ninety. He had blond hair and blue eyes and would have been much cuter without the scowl. The boys were all wearing their Granger caps and Ts, even Mr. Granger, though his T was stitched "Don" instead of "Delivery Boy." His fit him better when he'd first gotten them before he gained all that pandemic weight. Amelia's T was also an XL, great as a nightshirt, not so much as an official uniform unless she was working for a tent maker.

When Don told her to go back inside and put on her uniform, she said, "May I have a smaller one, please, Mr. Granger?"

The boys laughed. She made sure Toby Granger hadn't stuck a "Kick Me" sign on her when he patted her on the back and wished her good luck. Ricky called her a moron and launched back into what they'd been arguing about before she butted in—someone called Amos. As it happened, in addition to being the nephew of the village librarian, Ricky was also the oldest and longest-tenured of the delivery boys. When he was eleven, he was the newbie and only got the stops the older kids didn't want: the crummy tippers and the light baggers who never ordered more than twenty bucks in groceries at a time. Ricky said he paid his dues, and now, he was top dog. Now, it was his turn to get Amos, not some newbie girl, especially when there were hardly any stops anymore.

After listening to Don present management's view on who got what stops, which boiled down to if you don't like it, you can quit, Amelia returned to her unresolved agenda item. "A small would be great if you have one, Mr. Granger."

The boys laughed again. She checked her hair to ensure she hadn't picked up a hitchhiker on the way to the market.

Ricky said, "Idiot, can't you read? He's Don."

Don told him to stop it. "Amelia, the boys call me Don here at work. You know, like it says on the shirt?"

"Yes, sir. Do you have a small?"

The short answer was "no." The long answer was when Don first conceived of Granger's Special Delivery, he'd purchased a carton of XL T-shirts and another carton of one-size-fits-all baseball caps. He still had a half dozen or so left of each and wasn't buying any more until he used them up. Amelia put hers on over Ruth's top and donned her cap; at least that fit.

Don introduced her to the group and then introduced the boys to her, beginning with Ricky. She said hello, and he said whatever. Next was the leprechaun, Jacks. He was eleven and had only been there a few weeks. He seemed nice enough, quiet, and on the short side next to the Jolly Green Giant, who was about a foot taller than Ricky and an inch or two more than Don. Don introduced him as Little John. He was twelve and had been there since the beginning of the summer. Don called him "Little John" because everyone called his father Big John, even though Little was already bigger than Big. Little John's hair was longer than Amelia's mom would let any of her brothers grow theirs, and though he was not yet a teen, he had a breakout on his chin that he hid with the wrong tone of acne cream.

With the formalities out of the way, Ricky returned to the bone he'd been picking. "It's not fair, Don. Amos should be mine. I'm the oldest. I'm next after Petey."

Amelia wanted to know who Amos was and why it was such a big deal. According to Ricky, the answer was, "butt out, it's none of your business," but as Amelia quickly pointed out, "Aren't you mad because I have Amos? Doesn't that make it my business?"

"It makes you a moron," Ricky said. "So, shut up."

"I said, stop it, Ricky," said Don. "It's done. Amos is hers. If you don't like it, go home and cool off. I'll give your stops to one of the other boys."

Amelia offered to take them. Don told her to tuck in her shirt. She looked sloppy. She countered that it already looked sloppy, drooping off her shoulders like that, and it was too wide around the neck and had too much fabric to tuck in without it bunching around the waist.

The other boys found Ricky's whining baby impression of her amusing.

Growing up with three older brothers and Ruth, who didn't have time for it and wouldn't understand anyway, Amelia was used to it. "Ricky," she said. "Making fun of me doesn't change the fact that the shirt's too big. Tucked in or not, the top will still look stupid."

"*You're* stupid," he said.

Don said, "It's all cotton. Have your mother wash it in hot water and throw it in the dryer on high. Do it a couple of times. It'll shrink. If it doesn't, have her pin it for you. In the meantime, do you want to change out of that shirt you're wearing underneath? The restroom is inside. It's going to warm up. You'll thank me later."

Ricky told her she looked dumb. He was right about the look, but living with four seventeen-to-twenty-year-old siblings, two parents, and Grandpa Ralph, she wasn't dumb enough to leave Ruth's precious top anywhere unprotected with him around. "I'll keep it on if it's alright with you," she replied.

"Suit yourself," said Don, "but tuck it in. I can't have my boys running around looking sloppy. It reflects badly on us."

She tucked the T in. It bunched around the waist, as she had said it would. So, instead of looking sloppy, she looked like she was wearing a deflated balloon, but at least everyone could see the phone in her pocket again.

Little John asked what kind it was.

When she told him it was a smartphone, Ricky said, "He's asking what kind, moron."

"I told him what kind," she replied. "If he wanted to know what brand, he should have said so."

"How'd you get a phone?" said Little John.

When Amelia pointed out that she was in seventh grade and seventh graders needed phones, he said, "No way. I'm in seventh, too. I go to Lambert Middle. What about you?"

She and Mom usually went out on the deck for her lessons or to one of their favorite spots near the ocean if the weather was nice. When it wasn't, they'd sit in the living room when Grandpa Ralph wasn't in there smoking, or they'd work at the kitchen table if he were, or she'd go up to the attic to study alone where it was just her and generations of stuff. Anywhere — that was where she went to school.

"I homeschool," she said. "Technically, I attend Lambert Middle School like you, and technically, Miss Melucci is my teacher, but she's more my advisor, and I work mostly independently. Mom does the actual teaching, and I go at my own pace. There are two Johns in the class. Which one are you?"

"John Taylor."

She extended her hand. "I'm Amelia Gardiner. It's nice to meet you in person, John Taylor."

The handshake seemed awkward despite her following Mom's instructions on introducing herself professionally to a coworker.

Ricky said, "He already knows who you are, idiot.

Don just told you."

"He didn't say my last name, Ricky."

"Like there's more than one Amelia in seventh grade?"

"There are two. It was the country's fourth most popular girl's name when I was born, after Olivia, Emma, and Charlotte."

Little John shrugged. "It wouldn't have mattered. I don't pay much attention during roll call."

"That's okay," she said. "I'll be in eighth soon anyway. Does everyone call you Little John?"

"Just here."

"What do people call you when you're not here?"

"Just John," he shrugged.

"Is it okay if I call you just John?"

"Sure." Little John had a nice smile except for that missing tooth on the one side she hadn't noticed before because he'd been smiling with his mouth closed.

Instead of letting it go, Ricky insisted, "He's Little John," choosing to die on that hill.

Amelia said, "Calling him Little John is like calling me Amelia the Giant."

"That's what Don calls him."

"Okay, you can call him that, and I'll call him John. What difference does it make?"

"It's like saying Cliffs Climb is Ricky's Climb. It's not my climb. It's stupid."

"Cliffs Climb isn't named after a person. Your analogy doesn't work."

Ricky wasn't interested in the finer points of

apostrophes and told her to get lost before again telling Don that giving her Amos wasn't fair. Don reminded them all that Saturday was the busiest day of the week, and it was time they all got to work. If they still had a problem, they could turn in their Granger Market Ts and ball caps and go home. He'd find someone else.

"The stops are posted on the board," he said. "Let's get to work."

"What about me?" Amelia asked.

"Any questions, ask Little John," said Don. "He's your partner for today."

Note from the Author

She's off to a fantastic start! In fifteen minutes, Amelia managed to get the store's best tipper, make an enemy for life, and be partnered with someone almost two feet taller than her and intimidating enough to make even Ricky think twice about trying anything. Oh, that Ricky. Do you remember when you said your first bad word? I do. I might have been ten. It was after a little league game, and a few of us hung around in the dugout trying to decide who was to blame for our most recent trouncing. Someone's older brother said we were shitty. I had no idea what that meant, except it sounded worse than terrible. I went home after that and was playing solitaire in the family room, bemoaning my shittiness by saying "shit" over and over again, when Mom appeared out of nowhere with the announcement that shit was what bears did in the woods, and she didn't want to hear it coming out of my mouth again. She never did, and I'm more careful about where I step in the woods now. Until next time.

4) The Board

The "board" was a blackboard mounted to the wall outside Don's office in the store's back corner. He'd salvaged it and a box of colored chalk from the trash back when one of the local schools was getting rid of them. Abigail, the artist in the family, had masking-taped a three-column grid onto it. Above that, she wrote the word DELIVERIES using adjacent complementary colors of chalk that vibrated if you looked at them too long. And she'd shellacked the whole thing afterward in case anyone got any funny

ideas. The first two columns in the grid were
numbered 1 through 5 and 6 through 10. There had
been a third column for 11 through 15, but Don un-
taped it because it hadn't been used in a while and
looked embarrassing, always empty. That left the space
an open canvas for drawings of robots and superheroes
that weren't half bad, a message to Ricky from Mrs.
Granger to stop by before he left for the day, and a
heart Jacks had drawn in red chalk with the word
"Bern" inside. Ricky was happy to clarify for Amelia
that Jacks didn't misspell "burn" because it didn't mean
heartburn, moron. It was Bernhart, his last name.

Little John filled Amelia in on the basics. Don
posted the stops as the orders came in, starting with
number 1. Some days, he didn't post any. On
Saturdays, though, there were always at least five or
six. This particular Saturday, there were six. Each had
the customer's name, address, and phone along with
the initials of the boy Don picked to deliver there. Stop
number 6 was Amos Evers, 10 Cliffside Terrace, with
no phone number and the initials A and LJ beside it.
They had two other stops on the board. J had one, and
R had two. Stops 2 through 6 had green check marks
beside them. Number 1 had the only red check mark. It
was one of Ricky's. After Amelia guessed incorrectly
why one of his had a red check, Little John explained
that green meant one boy could handle it. "Red" meant
it was more than one bag and might take two. They
had three bags between them because he could carry
more than the others, all three if she wanted. That she

understood, declining the offer, but having a red and a green, Ricky was carrying at least three. She didn't see how he could do that but didn't ask for an explanation.

"I figured we'd split the tips 50-50," Little John said. "I mean, if that's okay with you, Amelia."

Amelia liked her name. It was her grandmother's, the one she never knew, but it wasn't her name on the board.

"Call me A," she said. "And 50-50 sounds good."

They shook on it.

He shrugged. "Okay."

"Can I call you LJ?"

"I thought you wanted to call me John?"

Ricky and his attitude hadn't strayed far. "You don't call guys by their initials just because it's on the board, moron."

"I have a name, Ricky," she said, "and it's not Idiot or Moron. It's A."

Proving both cute and clever despite the perpetual scowl, Ricky replied, "Is that your whole name, A Hole?"

"Grow up, Ricky."

Ricky spit in her general direction. "What's that supposed to mean?"

"It's English. It means, 'grow up.'"

Ricky might have had more growing up to do, but for the moment, he was five feet one inch and weighed ninety pounds. Amelia was eleven inches shorter and half his weight.

"You think I won't hit a girl?" he said.

"It's not my fault I'm a girl, Ricky, and it shouldn't make any difference anyway. So, grow up."

When you're ten, the youngest of five, and your next older sibling is your seventeen-year-old annoying sister whose put-downs come in more than one language, you grow up fast. Ricky Finnerty wasn't an only child; he was just acting like one.

"He gave you Amos," he said.

"I get it, Ricky, but it's Mr. Granger you should be mad at, not me." The problem was he still was mad at her, and considering it was either give him Amos or make an enemy for life on her first day, she said, "Okay, if it means that much to you, I'll trade you for your red. It's Tanner's. Mr. Tanner and my dad are friends. He stops there for breakfast sometimes on the way to the docks, sometimes on the way home, too. And Mrs. Tanner is nice, except she calls me Reds, which I hate. Their order must be huge if it's a 'red.' I'll bet we get a bigger tip than you will from Amos, no matter how good a tipper he is. Plus, Tanner's is just down the street. Cliffside Terrace isn't. It's up on the cliffs. We'll be back for more stops before you get there, but if it makes you happy, let's trade."

Grandpa Ralph always said, "If you agree, you shake on it," so she extended her hand.

He slapped it away. "I didn't ask for your life story. And Tanner's is mine."

"Then, you can't have Amos. You've already got more than you can carry."

"Think again, loser," he said, shoving his phone in

her face. "Check it out."

It turned out Mrs. Finnerty was right about her nephew saving up his hard-earned tip money. Ricky had wheeled into town that morning on his brand-new fire-engine-red ten-speed bike with side baskets. His dad kicked in some, and Ricky still owed him back, but he had his wheels now. A red and a green were no sweat. He could've done Amos, too. He should've. It was his turn.

Ricky was a shover. After shoving his phone in her face, he pushed her out of the way and took a photo of the board, another important use of a phone that she would have to bring up with Mom at her earliest opportunity. Jacks was busy copying the name and address of his only green into the little notebook he'd brought in place of the phone he couldn't afford, complaining about how unfair it was that Don only gave him one green. That became an argument with Ricky and then a shoving match.

Don was in his office with the door closed, but walls have ears — big ones when they're only half-walls and there's no ceiling. Don always regretted not spending some of that COVID relief money on an actual enclosed space to replace the glorified cubicle he'd inherited with the market. He stormed out of his office and separated the two. He had work to do, and they had work to do, and it was time they all got to it.

"Consider this a wake-up call, boys," he said. "A boy with a bike can deliver more groceries faster. It's the future of the delivery business. Think about it."

"I thought drones were the future of the delivery business," said Amelia.

"You know what I mean."

"That we could lose our jobs if we don't get a bike?"

"That's not what I'm saying, Amelia."

"Yes, sir, but if I'm supposed to call you Don, could you please call me A when I'm here so it matches the board?"

In reply, Don pointed her into his office.

Note from the Author

Don simply wants to explain to Amelia how she should get along with others, specifically his ace delivery boy, Ricky, instead of squabbling with them on her first day. Right? He won't fire her four episodes into the story, right? She's only asking questions, pointing out holes in other people's logic, contradicting the boss, the usual things kids do around adults. Besides, Don gets his best fish on the cheap from her dad. His wife and her mother are friends. He can't just fire her, can he? We'll see.

5) Holding the Bag

Little John was waiting by the delivery table with their orders when Amelia returned from her meeting with Don. The delivery table was an old ping-pong table Mrs. Granger had picked up at a yard sale. She'd stenciled the numbers 1, 2, and 3 in three of the table's four quadrants to match the columns on the board. "Don" was stenciled in the fourth. That was for things she wanted him to remember to bring home.

"Simple, right?" said Little John. "What did he want?"

She checked her cell as if anyone would be messaging her on her brother's phone. Poor brother Ralphy, not only was he named after Grandpa Ralph, but at least two of his friends thought he was ghosting them, and she'd only had his phone since last night. When Amelia wanted to act cool, she acted like Ruth. Ruth was annoying but cool. "Is that what it's like being sent to the principal's office?" she said. "Just curious, being home-schooled and all."

"What did he say?"

She shrugged. "The usual, and he had some form for Mom and Dad to sign so he doesn't get sued."

Along with leftover T-shirts and hats, Granger's also had boxes of leftover brown paper shopping bags, all legally purchased with relief money, if anyone from the IRS was inquiring. Don bought them because reusable bags seemed like a bad idea during a pandemic, and he had gotten boxes and boxes of them because they were such a deal. Three of them were on the table. One was over-filled, but it looked like it would be okay if you didn't jiggle it too much. One was only half-filled, probably for someone picking up a few last-minute things. Bag number 6 in quadrant 3 was Amos' bag, complete with a cantaloupe on top.

"Amos is mine, right?" said Amelia, picking up the bag and steadying the melon that whoever packed the groceries should have packed at the bottom. One arm under, one arm around — despite having ignored Grandpa Ralph's advice on rain gear, she chose to follow it on how to hold a shopping bag without everything coming out the bottom.

"I can carry them all if you want," Little John said, picking up the other two bags and setting the half-empty one on top of the other to keep anything from falling out. He offered his free hand for Amos' bag.

She declined. They were only partners for the day. She had to find out if she could do it by herself. If she couldn't, she needed to look for another job.

"That's what Don said to you, isn't it?" he said.

"He's right. What good is a delivery boy who can't carry a bag?"

She set the bag down and snapped a selfie in front of the board, texting it to Ruth to show Mom.

Seconds later, Ruth messaged back, "Where's my top???" The three question marks meant she didn't understand why her little sister, who'd stolen her blouse, was not wearing it in the photo.

"It's under my uniform," Amelia messaged back. "I borrowed it. You weren't around."

"You stole it."

"I borrowed it."

"I'm telling Mom."

"I'll tell her about your boyfriend."

"I hate you."

"Hate you, too. Bye. Just show her the pic, pls."

Ricky and Jacks were long gone, and Don was staring at them through his office window. Amelia put the phone away and shifted Amos' bag to a safer position.

"You should repack that," Little John said.

"I can't. The principal's watching."

They left by the back door, took the alley to Broad, and cut through the cemetery into West Hook. Their first delivery was to the Grauls, who lived not far past the cemetery in a development of one-plan-fits-all homes that were less alike than they looked after World War II when first built. Amelia knew the Grauls, mainly through Dad's complaining about people who liked to call themselves fishermen but still hadn't learned how after forty years of trying. They had a daughter who was a little older than Amelia. She barely knew her except through church. The Graul's were one of Little John's regulars. They got the half-filled bag. He told her to wait on the street while he delivered it.

When he returned minus the stopper for his overstuffed bag, she asked how much the tip was. "I waved, but I don't think Mrs. Graul saw me."

"There wasn't any," he said.

"She didn't tip you?"

"Nope."

"Isn't she supposed to?"

"You don't ask the Grauls for money."

The fisherman who had managed to scrape by for forty years doing something he still hadn't learned how to do didn't have a boat at the moment. The family business was in dry dock up in Lambert. Mr. Graul was crewing part-time on a friend's boat to raise the money for the repairs, but it was hard work, and the pay was a lot less. In the meantime, Don gave them half a bag of free food weekly. Their tip was their thanks, and Amelia was welcome to as much of it as she wanted.

Their second delivery was to a much nicer house on a cul-de-sac of similar upscale homes in North Hook. Little John knew little about the family except that the man mowing the lawn in the back worked at the bank, and they didn't tip much. He figured around five percent, maybe a little more. Again, Amelia watched from the street. This time, he came back and handed her a dollar, her first dollar. Dad and Grandpa Ralph's first dollars hung over the mantle. That's how much they meant to them.

"That's it?" she said. "A dollar? The bill was $61.50."

"Yep."

"This isn't five percent, LJ. Five percent is $3.08 if you round up, which you should. Half of that is $1.54, not a dollar."

"She gave me two dollars."

"Ruth said, at Tanner's, if you leave less than twenty percent, the waiters will ask you what's wrong."

"That's what she gave me, Amelia."

"It's A," she corrected him, immediately regretting it. He told her to forget it. She asked if he'd said thank you, a legitimate enough question, but one implying it was his fault they'd only given him two dollars.

At least, that was how he took it. "Yeah, I did," he said.

The four cardinal virtues are prudence, justice, courage, and temperance. Persistence is not one of them because, at times, it only makes matters worse, as it did when she pressed him. "And you smiled?"

"Why are you asking me all these questions?" he said, loud enough to get the banker's attention. He waved a friendly hello to them from atop his riding mower.

"Because," said Amelia, "I read that people tip more when you're polite and smile."

"That's as 'more' as it gets for them, A. The rich don't get rich by giving money away."

"But we provide a valuable service."

"And that's all they think it's worth."

That first dollar looked so lonely in her hand. "How much does Amos tip? It must be a lot for Ricky to be such a pain about it."

"It's kind of up to you."

"What does that mean?"

"I was there last Saturday with Petey. Amos leaves a roll of bills in his mailbox. I've never seen so many fifties plus a jar of change. You're supposed to take what you need for the order and figure out your own tip."

"No way."

"Yes, way."

"Ruth said one of you would try pranking me on my first day. It's your way of letting me into your club. Did I pass?"

"I'm not pranking you, A. Don told you to take the

money from the mailbox, didn't he?"

"He never said take what I want."

Amelia once had to grade her own art project. She didn't want to, but everyone in the class had to. She gave herself an F. She said, "Mr. Granger said to put the groceries on the chair, take the money and tip, and don't ring the bell till I'm ready to go, and definitely don't wait for him to answer the door; just leave. He never said I had to decide my own tip."

"Well, you do."

"What percent did you take? Was it more than twenty? Please, say it was more than twenty."

"I don't know what it was. Petey never showed me the bill. He just told me how much to take."

"So, how much was it? Assuming today's bill is average, we'll subtract it from what Petey said to take, and the leftover will be our tip."

"I don't remember."

"What about your share? Do you remember that? We'll double it."

"I didn't get a share."

"You weren't splitting 50-50?"

Little John shook his head.

"LJ, why did Petey quit?"

"He didn't quit. He got fired."

Note from the Author

Servers don't usually hand you the check with the tip filled out, and street musicians don't usually leave their guitar cases open beside them with a sign saying how much it costs to hear their version of "Country Roads." It's not up to them. But what if it were? It's a long climb up those cliffs. One could justify a thirty, maybe even forty percent tip for that. Amelia will have plenty of time to think about it.

6) Cliffs Climb

The main north-south highway was Route 5. Initially, it was a trade route that connected villages and towns along the coast. The traffic light at the corner of Main and Route 5 was where the open-air fish market was before Jasper Northside's great-grandfather built the Northside Docks. When the State constructed a bigger and better Route 5 miles west, bypassing Hook, Hook's Route 5 became Business Route 5. To further complicate things, the fork in the road at the scenic route sign just south of Brook Lane on Business 5 was designated Alternate 5, though no one called it that. The road's official name was Lambert High Road, but no one called it that either. Everyone just called it the cutoff. It was the winding two-lane scenic way around Hook to Lambert. The people who traveled it either lived on the cliffs or came for the view of the inlet. Were you a Granger's delivery boy, such as Ricky Finnerty, and you were delivering groceries to someone on the cliffs, such as Amos, you would hop on your bike, take Main down to the light at Business 5, go south to the cutoff, and make the steep climb to Cliffside Terrace in 10th gear — a piece of cake. If you were hoofing it like Amelia and Little John, you'd take the shortcut — Cliffs Climb.

Around the time of the War of 1812, before there was a cutoff and a Business Route 5 when, for some reason, the quaint little fishing village of Hook by the Sea considered itself a legitimate target of the British Royal Navy, the villagers fashioned an escape route up the cliffs just in case. Amelia's seventh-grade civics book described how the villagers created a path in three switchbacks using the natural irregularities in the granite cliffs. It was a steep climb, and they called it Cliffs Climb because you were climbing the cliffs. Simple enough, but unfortunately, the original sign posted at the foot of the path instead read Cliff's Climb. For a long time, stories circulated about the heroic Cliff, a fisherman who had single-handedly saved the villagers from the British by leading them up the cliffs to safety. The village only discovered the error after someone important enough to sue the infamous Cliff's descendants for negligence fell and broke their leg coming down. The lawyers never found Cliff or his heirs but did uncover the original proclamation naming the trail. As the only remaining defendant in the case, the village settled the suit, corrected the sign, added railings and guardrails, and fixed the civics books.

"So that's supposed to be funny?" said Little John, pondering the Cliffs Climb sign on which someone had graffitied an apostrophe.

"It's historical," said Amelia, awkwardly one-handing the groceries while taking a selfie in front of the sign. She messaged it to Miss Melucci instead of Ruth, who was still mad at her and wouldn't get it anyway.

Mission accomplished, they headed up the trail. It was wide enough to walk side-by-side at the start, but she took the lead when it began to narrow, and neither wanted to be outside. They stopped for a breather at the first switchback. Don was right about it warming up, and Amelia almost wished she'd taken his advice and left Ruth's top to the vagaries of Ricky.

Little John hocked a magnificent loogie over the edge and watched it splatter on the rocks below.

"Congratulations," said Amelia. "I wish I could say I'm grossed out, but I have brothers. So LJ, Amos' bill is $62.53. Twenty percent of $62.53 is twelve-fifty, rounded down, of course. Half of that is $6.25." She scowled, disappointed that she'd done the calculation the long way instead of just moving the decimal point one place to the left to yield ten percent. "What do you think? How's $6.25 each sound for having to scale Mt. Everest?"

"A lot better than nothing," he replied.

"Why was Petey fired?"

"I don't know. Ricky just said he was."

"Oh," she said. "Was us splitting 50-50 your idea?"

Little John pled guilty as charged and asked if it was still okay.

"It's definitely okay," said Amelia. "We should be pooling the tips and splitting them equally anyway like Ruth said they do at Tanner's. She works part-time in the kitchen, theirs, not ours. She's never around to help out in ours. The point is, there shouldn't be any fighting over who gets what customer."

"Especially when it's Ricky," he said in a way that surprised her.

He hadn't rolled his sleeves up tight to show off his muscles like Ricky. He hadn't called her an idiot or a moron or otherwise tried to intimidate her. He was so big he didn't need to do anything.

"Are you afraid of him?" she said.

He didn't look afraid. "I don't like fighting," he said.

She took his non-answer as reassuring. "Are you saving for a phone, too?"

"What makes you think I want one?"

"Don't you?"

"I don't know. Are you looking to upgrade yours?"

"This isn't mine. It's my brother, Ralphy's. He's

letting me use it while he's out on the boat with Dad."

"That's nice."

"Mom made him. I'm saving for one of my own. That's why I'm working. It won't be as nice as this, but it'll be good enough to finally get connected to the real world. The one I picked costs $55.65 a month for the first two years until the phone is paid for. After that, it's $15 a month plus tax."

"Sounds like a lot."

"It's only $12.84 a week for two years and $3.46 a week after that, but I'll need to save enough first to make up the difference every month."

"Are you sure you want to split the tip?"

She nodded. "It'll take longer, but it's fair. We should get going."

Little John was over three times Amelia's weight, and he pulled too hard when he offered a hand to help her up. She jerked forward and, despite being the only one in her family able to juggle three balls at once, failed to catch Amos' cantaloupe as it launched from the bag and bounced over the edge. They watched it splatter on the rocks below in an awesome and terrifying display.

It was agreed it was nobody's fault except whoever packed the bag. The question became what to do about it. Their choices were to go back or go on. Amelia's vote was to press on. Little John wasn't so sure, but they were over halfway there, and that wet spot on the bag meant something cold inside was defrosting. Having it spoil because they took too long would be worse than shorting the order and bringing Amos a replacement melon later, so his vote was to do both. He'd run back and get another, and she'd keep going.

"I'll catch up before you hit the top," he said.

"No, you won't."

"Wanna bet?"

"Grandpa Ralph says the only ones who bet are the ones with money to lose. What do you think Mr. Granger will do?"

Little John shrugged, "I'll just take another. Nobody will ever know."

"Toby will. I saw him taking inventory on a handheld. Every cantaloupe in the store has a barcode. It's how they ring them up at checkout and how they know if someone is stealing them."

"It's just a cantaloupe."

"It's stealing. I'll call Mr. Granger. He'll know what to do."

"Don't. He'll just get mad."

Amelia handed him her first dollar ever. It was never going over the mantle with Dad and Grandpa Ralph's. It was supposed to be going toward her phone, but instead, it was paying for damaged merchandise.

"Here's my half," she said. "They were a dollar ninety-nine. Pick out a good one. I'll wait for you at Amos'."

Note from the Author

Unfortunately, I can no longer claim that no melons were harmed during the telling of this story, but how about the price of cantaloupe? If cantaloupe is priced per pound, Don's must be hollow to be that cheap. But seriously, who knew two kids without parental supervision and having just met could actually reason through a problem and come up with a solution without pushing or shoving? I apologize for the hocking of a magnificent loogie during the climb. I know. It's gross. See you next time.

7) 10 Cliffside Terrace

Grandpa Ralph's knees were right. The wind shifted landward and jammed the storm down the inlet's throat. When Amelia reached the top, it was chilly on the cliffs without the sun and smelled like rain. Soon enough, it wouldn't just smell like rain; it would feel like it, and then it would be rain, and she'd get soaked. She hurried down the path from Cliffs Climb to the street and arrived at 10 Cliffside Terrace before LJ, noting the time to let him know later just how badly she'd beaten him.

Amos lived in the first house right after the path ended, an A-frame on a dead end. The siding was red, though mostly obscured behind the morass of vines overgrowing that side of the porch. One of them was poison ivy. The cottage had a front porch in similar condition, and wildflowers grew in the brick walkway leading up to it. The mailbox full of cash was nailed to the railing by the front door, in sight of the living room window from where LJ thought Amos was watching. The rusty metal folding chair by the door looked like it came from the same curbside as the ones Don set out for his boys in the delivery area.

The way the house was oriented, there would have been a clear view of sunrise over the inlet from the far end of the porch if not for the competing honeysuckle and clematis growing around the rails and up the posts, contending for every precious inch of sunlight. Grandpa Ralph would have had a fit, and Mom would have sketched the scene and done a beautiful watercolor showing how sad it looked, but it was a gold mine for a skilled yard worker such as herself. Amelia took a photo to show them later.

A white picket fence separated his yard from the coastal meadow running along the cliffs behind the house, though it was hard to tell where one started and the other ended when nobody had mowed the lawn in years. There was a tree in the backyard, tall enough to obstruct the view of the inlet from the second-floor windows. She wasn't sure what kind it was, but Grandpa Ralph would have called it dead enough to cut down. A swing dangled from its lowest limb by a single rope. She took another photo.

There was nothing to do but wait for LJ, so Amelia checked the time and sat down on the boulder that marked the official start of Cliffs Climb and the village's legal liability. When you have nothing to do and a phone, you have something to do. She looked up the difference between "house" and "cottage" and discovered it was somewhat a matter of opinion, though most agreed cottages were smaller. Amos' cottage was much smaller than their house, but they didn't have a front porch like his or that view of the cliffs.

She googled his address. The only hit that wasn't an ad was an obituary for Harry Bendix, who died when she was two. His wife of fifty-three years had died just three months before him. He left behind a daughter and her family. Amelia also found a county tax record showing Amos purchased the cottage barely a month after Harry's death.

Ruth had finally given up bugging her about her top, and the weather app that told her not to listen to Grandpa Ralph was now issuing a coastal flood advisory. She sent the photos she'd taken to Ruth.

"Show this to Mom," she messaged.

"No," was Ruth's reply.

"Your top is okay, Ruth. I promise. Can you please show her?"

Ruth replied with a turd emoji, which Amelia took as a no until Ruth messaged, "She wants to know where you are."

"Doing a delivery."

"She said where???"

"Cliffside Terrace."

"Now she wants to know why Mr. Granger would make you walk all that way."

"We didn't. We took Cliffs Climb."

"No, you didn't."

Amelia's emoji in reply said otherwise.

"Mom is going to kill you."

"Only if you tell her."

"Why shouldn't I?"

"I'll make it up to you."

"???"

"I'll take your turn tonight."

"It's already your turn."

"I took your turn last night because you were sick. Remember?"

"That makes it your turn tonight."

"No," Amelia said, waiting for the crickets to simmer down before texting, "Fine, but you have to promise."

"Okay."

"Say it, Ruth, or it's not a promise."

"I promise. Happy now?"

"Overjoyed. Thank you." Amelia put the phone away.

When she graduated fourth grade, they made everyone march up the aisle to accept their diplomas. She was first in line because she was the shortest, except for Margie, who wouldn't go first, not even for a dollar from the teacher. LJ wasn't coming, Ruth was blackmailing her, and it was starting to drizzle. She gave the time one last check as if it would make him get there any faster, picked up the groceries, and marched down the sidewalk and up the steps. Setting the groceries down in the chair by the front door, she texted Miss Melucci for advice about what to do next, given the order was missing a cantaloupe.

There was a noise inside. Whoever was behind the door was a wheezer. She rang the bell. No one answered.

"I have your groceries, Mr. Evers," she said and apologized that there was a problem with the order and she needed a few minutes to figure it out. A few turned into five, waiting for Miss Melucci to answer. She begged him for a little more time, and when that too passed with no reply, and there was still no sign of LJ, she gave up and said, "I lost your cantaloupe, Mr. Evers. I'm sorry. I should have been more careful. LJ said he'd be right back with another, but he's not. I have things you need to get in the fridge. Do you want me to leave the bag and come back later with it? I don't mind."

Sometimes, when she'd ask Grandpa Ralph a complicated question, she'd have to wait a bit before he answered, so she waited. When Amos still didn't say anything, she offered the alternatives of subtracting the melon from the bill and not taking any tip until she came back with another, or of not doing anything with the money until she returned with another, or whatever he wanted. It was entirely up to him.

The older man who startled them both by opening the door was frail, with blue-piercing eyes, grayish-red hair, and skin that hadn't seen the sun in a while. He wore a brown suit and leaned on a cane. He was older than Grandpa Ralph and taller than Amelia, though as bent over as he was, they were nearly face-to-face when he opened the door without warning.

"What do you want me to do, sir?" she said, looking down at his uncomfortable shoes to avoid his even more uncomfortable gaze. "I'm really sorry. There was an accident on the way up, and your cantaloupe fell out. LJ ran back to get another, and he should have been here by now, but he isn't. I'll get you another. I promise."

She glanced up. Amos' stare was unforgiving. She looked down again and begged him to say something, anything.

"Look at me when you speak," he said, his voice gravelly, his inflections akilter, as if he'd spoken those words in different sentences and stitched them together to make this new one. He repeated himself, this time lifting Amelia's chin. "I'm deaf," he said. "I read lips."

She knew how to sign a few simple phrases, including "I'm sorry," but either Amos didn't know sign language or she was doing it wrong. "Yes, sir," she said to his face. "What do you want to do?"

"About what?" he said, stern but not angry,

puzzled but not bothered.

"Your cantaloupe," she said. "I'll get you another."

"What cantaloupe?"

"The one that was in the bag. It should have been at the bottom, but whoever packed it put it on top. That's why it fell out when LJ pulled me up."

"What's all this nonsense about a cantaloupe, child?"

"I'm not a child, Mr. Evers. I'm ten. I've been ten for 157 days, which means I'll be eleven in 208 more because it's not a leap year."

"I apologize," he bowed, though he might have been tipping over. It was hard to tell. "Had I known you were that close to eleven, I would have addressed you otherwise."

"It's actually only 43% of the way." She reached out to shake his hand. "Nice to meet you, Mr. Evers. I'm A, your new delivery person."

"A what?" he said, staring that hand back where it belonged.

"Just A," she said. "The letter A. No period. It's not an abbreviation. It's my work name."

"And your real name is what? Abigail, Agnes, Astrid?"

"Amelia. It was the fourth most popular name the year I was born."

"I see," Amos said, preparing to pick up the bag of groceries—something, in his case, either done right or disastrously.

"What about your cantaloupe?" she said.

"I didn't order a cantaloupe."

"They packed it by mistake?"

"Look at the list if you don't believe me. I assure you, there was no cantaloupe on it."

There was no cash register receipt stapled to the outside of the bag, only a piece of paper on which Don had written the item total, tax, and grand totals. Amos said he was referring to his handwritten list, the one from which the order should have been packed, the list Little John neglected to mention that should have been stapled to the outside of the bag along with the bill, as it always was. Amelia looked through the bag. It wasn't inside either, and Amos kept no copy. Why should he? He insisted she take him at his word, assume the bill was correct, and take what was required, and next time, do it without bothering him.

Amelia picked up the grocery bag and handed it to him when he said he was ready. He thanked her and went back inside, leaving her alone on the porch with a mailbox full of money and some unfinished business. She found the change jar, next week's list, and the purple rubber-banded roll of bills inside. There was also a resident spider LJ hadn't mentioned. There was more than enough in that wad of cash for Amos' $62.53 and more than enough for a twenty percent tip. She could have taken a hundred percent and not even made a dent. There were enough fifties to get a phone, any phone she wanted, and much more. She counted out $62.53 and put the rest back.

The drizzle had turned to a downpour. The

weather app was now saying the storm was blowing
out to sea, though that growing expanse of blue sky in
the west would have confirmed it for Grandpa Ralph.
She was trying to decide whether to wait it out on the
porch or make a run for it when Amos opened the
door, startling her again.

He handed her a raincoat. "Take this," he said.

One of its sleeves was patched with duct tape, and
the zipper was broken. It was a little too big but no
more ridiculous-looking than Amelia's Granger T. The
coat had seen rough weather but looked good enough
in a storm. Amelia thanked him and told him she'd
return it later that afternoon.

"It doesn't belong to me," he said. "It belonged to
Harry and Harry's dead."

"Don't you want it back?"

"I didn't want it in the first place. It was in the hall
closet when I moved in."

"Okay," she said. "Well, thanks again. Sorry I
bothered you, Mr. Evers."

"Aren't you forgetting something?"

She had apologized at least twice and thanked him
more than that. That wasn't it, and the $62.53 was in
her pocket, wrapped up with next week's list, and she
still had Ralphy's phone in her other pocket.

"Your tip?" he said.

"I didn't take one."

"I noticed."

"I don't deserve one," she said and told him why,
starting with how she should have ensured the order

was correct before leaving the store. If she had just thought to do that one simple thing, she would have realized there wasn't a list to check against and would have gotten Mrs. Granger to run a register tape. They would have discovered the mistake before she ever left, none of this would have happened, and she wouldn't have bothered the one customer Mr. Granger said never under any circumstances to bother.

"I see," he said, admitting his instructions to Donald on that matter had been quite specific. "But even so, your services today were worth infinitely more than nothing."

According to Grandpa Ralph, Amelia sometimes took things too literally. This was one of those times. "Isn't everything infinitely more than nothing?" she said, explaining that calculating a percentage increase from zero to any real number requires dividing by zero, which is impossible. So it can only be infinitely more, or it doesn't make sense.

Amos had been frowning for so many years that it was hard to gauge his reaction. He said, "At least take enough to pay for the cantaloupe. If I know Donald, he'll want to be reimbursed."

"That's okay," she said. "We already bought one to replace it. LJ was supposed to be coming back with it, but he got caught in the rain. I hope Mr. Granger takes it back."

"And if he doesn't?" he said, gesturing toward the mailbox. "Take as much as you like."

"Why do you put all that money in there, Mr.

Evers? Aren't you afraid someone's going to steal it?"

"I don't care."

"What if I took it all?"

"I don't care," he said again.

Amelia wanted to ask why he watched her from the window, gave her a raincoat, and wanted to know why she wasn't taking a tip if he didn't care, but couldn't with his eyes boring a hole in her head, so she simply thanked him and left.

Note from the Author

The summer after my first year in high school, I worked as a valet at a Hilton Hotel. I picked up and delivered laundry, shoes, and dry cleaning to the hotel guests. We got paid tips plus barely enough for the train to and from the city. There were four of us. We had our Don and an eighteen-year-old version of Ricky. We had a board where Don put the jobs, and we argued over who got what when a big tipper was involved. And we got some big tippers: visiting sports teams, sometimes celebrities, and politicians. I rarely got the big tippers because I was a newbie, but I did okay. I think it's time Amelia got back to the store. It looks like rain.

8) Return to the Market

Though the coat proved rain-worthy, it had no hood. There was a zipper where one would attach, but that was it. The rain had stopped when Amelia got to Broad and Main, looking as beaten down as she felt. A storm in Hook Inlet can do that. It can also make Dad late getting back to port if he's weathering it somewhere far out on the ocean. She messaged Ruth, asking if they'd heard anything yet. They hadn't. The Jane was out of cell range and wasn't answering the ship-to-shore radio. Mom had the weather channel on, and Grandpa Ralph was in the living room praying to

St. Peter, even though he said this kind of thing happened all the time when he was captain.

Amelia turned off Main and went into the alley behind the market. Ricky and Jacks were there, hanging out under the awning, smoking. As soon as Jacks saw her, his cigarette went under the dumpster. Ricky took another drag before blocking her way to the backdoor.

"How much did you take?" he said, blowing smoke in her face.

"What do you care? Come on, Ricky. Let me through," she said.

He wasn't budging. "I want to know."

"It's none of your business."

He still wouldn't let her through, and she threatened to call 911, but shaking your brother's phone in a bully's face like that never ends well. Ricky yanked it out of her hand and wouldn't give it back. "Check this out, Jacks," he said. "There's a sticky note on the back because she's too dumb to remember the number."

True, it was a sticky note she'd written the number on, trimmed down so it wouldn't look too dorky, and scotch-taped to the back just in case, but not because she couldn't remember Ralphy's number. "Give it back," she said.

"Money first."

"What money?"

"If Don's giving you Amos, I want my cut."

Each week, Teacher-Mom gave Amelia a list of

words she had to learn to spell and use in a sentence. The word describing what Ricky was doing was on it that week. "That's extortion," she said, short but a sentence she would later report for credit. "How about I tell Don you're smoking, or should I just let you die of mouth cancer because you're not inhaling?"

"You think you're funny?" he said, flicking the cigarette at her.

"Quit it, Ricky," she said. "Give me back my phone."

"It's not your phone, moron. It's your brother's."

"He told you?" she said, surprised, betrayed, and a few other things.

Little John poked his head out the door. "Don wants to see us. He said, 'Right now.'"

Ricky made her work for it but finally gave her back the phone. Don was waiting for them in the Principal's office. He wanted to know what happened.

Her pink tennis shoes sloshed and squeaked when she walked, her pants were soaked up to her knees, and her hair looked like a bucket of water had been dumped over it. "I got caught in the rain, sir," she said, handing him the money. "Here's the $62.53 and next week's list. There was a mix-up with the order. Whoever packed it made a mistake."

"Moron," said Ricky. "Don packs all the orders."

"I looked up 'moron' just to be sure, Ricky," she said. "Mom doesn't put words like that on my vocab lists. It's literally a foolish or stupid person. And you're right. I'm a moron. I should have known better."

"You have a phone," said Don. "Why didn't you call? You had us worried sick."

LJ, the reason why she hadn't called, was doing everything but looking her way. "I didn't want to bother you," she said.

"So instead, you bothered the one customer I specifically told you not to bother?"

This time, Little John didn't look away. He said, "Mrs. Granger wanted to know why I was buying another cantaloupe, A. She checked the order, and there wasn't supposed to be one."

"I know," said Amelia. "I waited for you, LJ."

"I would have let you know," he said, "but you never gave me your number."

"You never said you had a phone, so why would I?"

"It was starting to rain…"

Don said, "I had to send Toby to fetch you in the van, but by the time he got there, you were gone. Now he's stuck in traffic on the cutoff."

She apologized and said it wouldn't happen again.

"It shouldn't have happened in the first place, Amelia."

"It didn't happen because of me, Mr. Granger. It happened because *someone* put a cantaloupe in the wrong bag. But it won't happen again because I'm going to check my orders from now on to make sure."

Glared at but not directly accused, Ricky denied everything, accusing Little John of sabotaging the bag while she was in the office getting schooled by Don.

"Why would he do that?" Amelia said.

And Ricky replied, "Because Don was giving Amos to him, not you. Why do you think Don had Petey take him up there to show him around? For the view?"

"Why *did* you fire Petey, Mr. Granger?" Amelia asked.

"I didn't. He quit because he's on the track team."

"Ricky told LJ he was fired," she said, a lie Ricky then claimed was a joke that Little John was dumb enough to fall for. She asked Little John why Don gave her Amos instead of him. He was next after Ricky, not her.

Little John didn't want to talk about it, but Ricky was happy to. "It's because he got caught stealing. Now, Don doesn't trust him."

"Amos caught me putting it back," Little John said in his defense, admitting his wrong and intention to undo it. "But it wasn't me who put that cantaloupe there. You did it to mess with her, Ricky."

"Is that why he didn't give Amos to you, Ricky?" said Amelia. "Because he can't trust you either?"

"Shut up."

"That's enough," said Don. He wasn't accusing Ricky, but he was looking his way. "Whoever did this owes the store $1.99. When I find out who it is, I'll hold you responsible. And if you do it again, you're fired."

"You have cameras everywhere," said Amelia, pointing to the one overhead in the rafters that wouldn't have been visible had Don's cubicle had a ceiling. "Check the footage. That'll tell who did it, or maybe he'll confess now and apologize to save you the trouble."

Don said, "If any of you have anything more to say, say it now." No one did, so he told everyone except Amelia to get back to work. Her, he asked to close the door and take a seat.

"Am I fired?" she said, unsure which answer she preferred.

"No, you're not fired," said Don.

"If this is about Ricky, sir, it's fine. Honest. I have brothers."

"How was he?" Don asked.

" He was just being a bully. I can handle it."

"I meant Amos. How was he?"

When Amelia was on the porch with Amos, she stayed between him and the steps in case he was some kind of a lunatic weirdo, and she needed to make a run for it. He'd never catch her once she was out in the open unless he was faking needing a cane.

"You were right," she said. "I bothered him. Even he said so. I'm sorry, Mr. Granger. I didn't mean to, but we figured out the problem, and he even gave me a raincoat. I didn't take a tip," she said, ending the list of mitigating circumstances that didn't appear to be making any impression.

"How did he look?" said Don. "Was he alright?"

"What do you mean, Mr. Granger?"

"Did he look sick?"

"He walks with a cane. Did you mean *that*?"

"No," Don said, seeming satisfied with her answer.

"Thank you, Amelia. You can go now."

She got up. "I'm sorry I got Toby stuck in traffic. Can I help with anything to make up for it?"

"It's not your fault, Amelia. The storm damaged the Milton Creek Bridge, and Business 5 will be closed until they can fix it. In the meantime, everyone is taking the cutoff. Toby said they're just now putting detour signs up, and a state trooper was there directing traffic. That was a heck of a storm. Have you heard from your father?"

"Not yet."

"I'm sure he's fine. Ask him to call me later, would you?"

"Yes, sir. Does this mean Jacks gets Amos? He's the only one left."

"No, you'll still deliver there."

"But I bothered him."

"I know."

"You told me not to."

"Just don't do it again. Three more deliveries came in. I put you with Little John."

"May I go home first and change, please?"

He checked his watch. "These can't wait, and by the time you get showered and changed, we'll be done for the day. I'll have him do it by himself."

Amelia looked at the clock on the wall behind him. "It's only one-thirty. I can be back by two or two-thirty at the latest, Mr. Granger. You don't close till six."

"You did well today, Amelia. Go home. Go outside and play. I'll see you tomorrow in church."

Note from the Author

This has Ricky written all over it. He who denied it supplied it—works for passing gas, and it works for passing blame. But what if Ricky's not lying? There is a chance he's right about LJ. Or maybe it was Jacks— eight episodes in and not a single line. You know it's always the quiet ones. Or maybe it was a simple mistake made when Don packed the order, and he's embarrassed to admit it, which explains his reluctance to check the CCTV footage. On the other hand, it's more likely he's too cheap to pay for the monthly monitoring service, and the cameras are just for show. Who knows? It's certainly a mystery, but one that will have to wait.

9) Getting Home in One Piece

Little John gave Amelia back her one dollar for the cantaloupe he never bought, and she started home a dollar richer for her three and a half hours of work. At twenty-eight cents an hour, a phone was a long way off. She waited for the light to change by the newly placed "Local Traffic Only" sign on Business 5, watching a flock of migrating birds feasting at the all-you-can-eat buffet left behind by the storm. The changing tide would be closing the kitchen soon, and they'd be moving on. A man who'd decided twenty dollars worth of scrap metal was worth a trip to the chiropractor was awkwardly loading a broken metal lobster trap into the back of his pickup. It had washed ashore during the storm without its marker buoy, making it impossible to return to whomever had lost it years ago when they were still lobstering in Hook Inlet. Ricky was coasting south on 5 no-hands toward the intersection, right down the middle of the deserted street.

Business 5 South was the quickest way home, but Amelia took the beach path. It's one thing to come home from your first day of work with a net profit of a dollar, and it looks like you've spent the last three and a half hours working the dunk tank at the County Fair. It's another to come home beaten up by Ricky. The path traced the inlet, keeping in sight of the ocean. There were no signs to mark the trail that wound among the rocks, crossed streets that dead-ended at the shore and went through people's backyards. It wasn't an official path. It was just the way locals went sometimes.

Ricky was waiting for her at a cross street farther down, smoking a cigarette.

"I saw you heading for the path," he said. "Why are you taking the long way?"

"What do you want, Ricky?"

"It's a free country."

"That doesn't mean you can beat people up."

"I had a stop up the street. I'm taking a smoke break."

"Smoking is bad for you."

"So is being a moron."

"Were they good tippers?"

"Not like Amos."

"Was it more than zero? Because that's what I got."

"That's your fault, stupid."

"Are you going back to the store?"

"Nah. Don said that was it," Ricky said, brushing cigarette ash off the handlebars of his shiny new bike.

"You should wax the frame," Amelia said. "Grandpa Ralph says it'll rust if you don't."

"Like I care about what your stupid Grandpa says. I didn't put that cantaloupe in your bag."

"Sure, you didn't."

"Jacks did it to get back at me."

"No way. Did Mr. Granger check the footage?"

"No, *Don* didn't check the footage. He didn't have to. Jacks blamed me for getting shafted on the orders today."

"You mean like you blame me?"

"He was messing with me, not you. Your bag had room on top. That was it. This had nothing to do with you."

"I don't know, Ricky. What did Mr. Granger say?"

"He's the one that fired him."

"He did?"

"Mrs. Tanner called. She found Amos' list in one of her bags when she was looking for the cantaloupe we shorted her. Don really let us have it, and the dumbass ran. That pretty much says it all."

"He hit him?"

"No, he didn't hit him. Adults go to jail for that."

"Wow. I can't believe it was him."

"Don made me run another one up to the tavern and apologize. He said I should offer my tip back, but I'm not stupid like you."

"I counted over five hundred dollars in that mailbox, Ricky. That's more than enough for a new bike. How *did* you afford that bike? Your aunt said you've been saving your tip money since you were eleven, yet I distinctly remember you complaining to Don that it was finally your turn to make some real money, and he wouldn't let you. Did he catch you stealing, too?"

"You have no clue how much it sucks hoofing groceries around this dump and getting zip for it."

"I have a pretty good idea."

"I've been doing that for three years, moron."

"How much did you take, Ricky?"

"I told you. Nothing."

Amelia could think of a million reasons why Don wouldn't let Ricky anywhere near Amos, each involving some form of criminal activity, but realized she'd mistakenly assumed it was Don not letting him.

She said, "You're acting like you got gypped out of Amos because you were caught stealing instead of just saying your parents won't let you? That's lame, Ricky."

"Shut up."

"Is it because they don't want you taking Cliffs Climb because they're afraid you'll fall?"

"I said, shut up."

"If you want Mr. Granger to convince them it's okay, why don't you try being nice? Grandpa Ralph says it works better on adults."

Ricky dropped the kickstand and got off his bike. "You better not tell anyone."

"I won't if you stop hassling me about Amos."

"I need that money."

"You've got your bike. Are you saving for a new phone, too?"

His was nice, but he could do better.

"I owe people," he replied.

"You owe people? You must watch the same shows as Grandpa Ralph."

The only thing between his fist and her face was his bike. He started around it, and she circled the other way. "I'll tell you what," she said. "I'll ask Mr. Granger… I mean, Don, to talk to your mom. He'll listen to me. He likes me."

"He told me you're a pain in the ass."

"No, he didn't. Look, Ricky, I don't want Amos. I just want to work, and I really need a phone. Is that too much to ask?"

He stopped. She did, too.

"You'd really do that for me?" he said.

"Stop calling me names and be nice for a change."

"It's easier just to beat you up," he said. Sleeves rolled tight, butt flicked in Amelia's general direction, and cigarette pack secure; Ricky cracked his knuckles and made his move. Amelia took off as fast as her soggy pink tennis shoes could carry her and didn't look back until she was down by the water and out of breath. Ricky was back on the dunes laughing.

Note from the Author

Kids like Ricky aren't born thinking it's funny to scare the crap out of someone half their size. They learn it by playing peekaboo. That's right. It's our fault. We taught them that doing something scary and surprising could be funny, too. Ricky is simply taking that lesson to heart and running with it into extortion, racketeering, and other assorted felonies for which he could be tried as an adult if he doesn't watch himself. But don't give up on him just yet. Give it a few more episodes. See you next time…

10) Mom

She was born Martha Smith, but everyone called her Mom, even Dad. He picked the habit up because it was less confusing for everyone. Mom was forty when she had Amelia. They were the only two in the family with red hair and freckles, though Mom's wasn't as red as it used to be and had a little gray in it now. She grew up in a mill town in the foothills of the Appalachian Mountains, where she met Bernie Gardiner when she was young and impressionable, and he was just out of the service, hiking the Appalachian Trail. Her recollection of how they met was that he took a wrong turn and came to the house asking for directions. His version was slightly different because Army rangers never get lost, but in either case, they fell for each other hook, line, and sinker. They eloped, married, and moved to Hook because living by the ocean sounded so much more romantic than getting up at six each morning to work in a mill for the rest of their lives.

Their dream didn't include the associated realities of moving in with Bernie's parents because, starting out, they couldn't afford a place of their own. It also didn't include staying there, even when they could, to care for Grandpa Ralph after Grandma Jane died. Their dream left out a few other details, too, such as getting up long before six so the fishermen in her family could be on the water for the sunrise catch and worrying when they didn't come home on time.

When Amelia got home, Mom was dozing on the back deck with a book in her lap. Grandpa Ralph was napping in his chair in the living room, and Ruth was long gone. Amelia showered, changed, and started a load of laundry before joining her.

"Hi, Mom," she said, dropping into the chair beside her, startling her. "What are you reading?"

"A trash novel," Mom replied, closing the book over her pencil and next week's vocabulary list. The challenge of the weekly vocabulary lists was to use each word in a sentence and, for extra credit, to use the sentence in a conversation.

"Mother," said Amelia, "I know you're a voracious,

omnivorous bookworm, but really?"

"You weren't supposed to see that."

"Mom, I just used two of next week's words in one sentence. Don't I get extra credit?"

"Do you know what they mean?"

"You like to read a lot about everything."

"I'm changing the list before I give it to you Monday, and no more peeking, Amelia."

"I've decided to go by A now if that's okay. It's my work name. I like it."

"It's better than Mel."

"I still like Lia, but everyone always made me spell it."

"Well, there aren't any more letters left. If you don't like A, I guess it's back to Amelia. How did it go today?"

How it went started and ended with Amos and his novel approach to tipping. Amelia left out the name-calling, intimidation, bullying, extortion, betrayal, embarrassment, and disappointment over only making a dollar. Amos was hers now, and her first real payday was next Saturday.

The day was as warm, the air was dead still, and Mom looked tired. She'd been up since four-thirty.

Amelia said, "Did Ruth show you the photo? You should do a painting of it."

Mom yawned. "She did. I almost didn't recognize the place. We were there for the Bendix wake. You were two. Who did you say lives there now?"

"Amos Evers. He's deaf. I'm his delivery person

now."

"That's very descriptive."

"Mom, Amos is old, walks with a cane, and is a shut-in. He doesn't have a phone or a car. Granger's has been delivering there since he moved in. He reads lips, and he puts the money in his mailbox. He told me to take as much as I want for my tip."

"How much did you take?"

"Do you remember that art project you made me grade?"

Mom did. She also remembered telling Amelia she'd been too critical of her work. "You didn't take any tip at all?" she said.

"I messed up, Mom."

Mom asked, "Doesn't it seem strange that he would let you take what you want?"

"He says it's because he can't be bothered. It must be nice."

"Did you try signing with him?"

"I tried to say sorry, but I don't think I did it right."

"Did he laugh?"

"I don't think Amos laughs."

"That's the second time you've called him that. Is that what you call him?"

"We all do, just not to his face."

"So that's where you went when you took Cliffs Climb instead of the cutoff?"

"Mom, it takes forever that way. Are you mad?"

"Should I be?"

"Maybe. Sorry. I probably should have called first

to make sure it was okay."

"Probably."

"But it was totally safe."

"It was raining."

"Mom, I only slipped once coming back down, but I was holding onto the rope. It was no big deal. Really."

"I'm not sure you're old enough to make that decision alone, sweetie."

"When will I be?"

"Do you want the legal answer or my answer?"

"Are they the same?"

"How about we walk it together tomorrow after church so I can see for myself. Then, we'll decide together whether or not it's totally safe."

"I'm taking Ruth's turn tonight," said Amelia. "Again."

"I heard. I hope she's feeling better. I don't like her missing school."

"What's for supper?"

In the Gardiner household, ask what's for supper, and Grandpa Ralph will tell you it was fish. It was just a matter of what kind and how it was cooked, except on Sundays when supper was meat and potatoes because that's a proper Sunday supper like Grandma Jane used to make.

Mom answered, "The trout your father traded some good menhaden for. It's been in the freezer too long. It needs to be used up."

"It looked gross. Let's make something else. I think

the leg of lamb has thawed out."

"It had better be."

"We should use some of it tonight."

"Sweetie, you know the lamb is for Grandpa Ralph's Sunday supper. It takes hours to roast, and I have no idea when your father will walk through that door. All I know is he said not to hold dinner if he isn't home by seven."

"You heard from him?" Amelia said, a silly question, given Mom wouldn't have been asleep in a chair with a book in her lap otherwise.

Mom nodded, but relief didn't look that different from worry. "They're alright," she said. "They got caught in it, but they're alright. Your father said it was a good catch, so they'll be there awhile, taking care of it."

"Let's surprise him. We'll make lamb stew. He loves lamb stew, and it won't take the whole leg. There will be plenty left for tomorrow. No one will even notice."

"We already have a supper plan for tonight."

"Mom, did you know that seventy-one percent of our suppers last month were fish? I've been keeping track."

"I didn't know the exact number, but I would have guessed whatever 5/7s works out to."

"It's 71.43% rounded."

"Only you, Amelia," Mom smiled.

Amelia frowned. "Could you please call me A, Mom?"

"I'm trying, dear. It took awhile with the others, too."

Mom looked tired. She was tired. She deserved a break. They all did. It had been a rough day for everyone, even Ruth. A family bucket of chicken with all the sides from the Stop-N-Shop would have been just the thing, but Dad didn't catch buckets of chicken. He caught fish, and they ate it 71.43% of the time.

Note from the Author

I could go for a bucket of chicken with all the sides right now. Did you know that the first chain convenience store in the United States opened in Dallas, Texas, in 1927 and eventually became 7-Eleven? True enough, but it wasn't until the 1960s that chains began adding gas stations, and gas stations began adding convenience stores until they essentially became the same thing. Even tiny fishing villages like Hook have one. Cars need fuel. People need fuel, too, even when dinner is only a hook, line, and sinker away. It's time for supper. I'm hungry.

11) Suppertime

Seven o'clock came and went. Dad and Amelia's brothers were still at the docks, so they ate without them. There was Mom, who seemed more worried than usual; Amelia, who was starving; Ruth, who wasn't feeling so hot; and Grandpa Ralph, who took one bite of the trout and declared it spoiled.

Miraculously feeling so much better, Ruth volunteered to go get fast food if someone else paid for it and did it soon because she wasn't allowed to drive at night yet, and it would soon be nine o'clock. Amelia offered to kick in her share, everything she earned that day, all one dollar of it. Mom suggested the leftover cod from the day before, which would soon go the way of the trout if they didn't use it. Grandpa Ralph told them it was almost Sunday, and he wasn't in the mood for leftover cod. He gave Ruth the cash to get one of those family buckets of chicken with all the sides, the one the kids like — his treat.

Grandpa Ralph had sixty-five more years of experience figuring things out than Amelia, and he was always happy to share the wisdom of the ages with anyone who would listen. Amelia always did, and she didn't mind how often he told the same story or offered the same advice. He'd been doing it all her life. It was just a part of him, like his big hairy hands or his self-cut thin gray hair, except for that patch in the back he couldn't see in the mirror. Grandma Jane used to tidy that spot up for him. Mom did it now. Grandpa Ralph always smelled like tobacco and was never without his trusty pipe, even though he wasn't supposed to smoke in the house. Grandma Jane would have made him clean up his act, but she wasn't there anymore. Her ashes were in an urn in his bedroom closet.

After getting stuck washing *and* drying the dishes after dinner because Ruth felt suddenly ill again, Amelia found him in the living room in the dark, nursing his favorite corncob, today's County Gazette lying open in his lap.

"Grandpa Ralph," she said, opening a window,

"you know you're not supposed to smoke in the living room."

There were many things Ralph Gardiner wasn't supposed to do. He wasn't supposed to be a fisherman for almost fifty years. He wasn't supposed to marry Jane Williams. He wasn't supposed to drive anymore, and he definitely wasn't supposed to smoke in the living room.

"When's that son of mine going to fix the chimney?" he said.

"I don't know," Amelia shrugged. She opened another window.

"You're letting in the flies," he said, "and you're making it chilly. If I wanted to smoke outside, I'd go outside."

Grandma Jane's afghan was on the floor and belonged on the back of her chair on the other side of the broken fireplace or on Grandpa Ralph's lap under the County Gazette. She put it back on his lap. "You're stinking up the house, Grandpa Ralph."

"The sooner he fixes that chimney, the sooner we can open the flue and light a fire. Then, maybe I can smoke in my own house again without being pestered all the time." He tapped the pipe in the ashtray and crushed the smoldering ashes with a yellow-stained thumb. "Satisfied?"

"Mom said you could smoke out on the deck."

"It's cold out."

"She said it's either that or you give everyone heart disease and lung cancer."

"She didn't say that. You did."

"Grandpa Ralph, it's everywhere."

"I don't smell anything, and close those windows. If you make it just as cold inside, I may as well smoke right here."

She readjusted the afghan on his lap. "Grandpa Ralph?"

"What?" he said, squinting at her over his half-lenses.

"Why do you smoke?"

"I like it. I want to."

"Can I do things that are bad for me and hurt others just because I want to?"

"No."

"Why not?"

"Because I said so."

"Is that the only reason?"

"No. It's complicated."

"But what if I want to smoke a pipe?"

"You're too young."

"But what if I want to?"

"I said you're not old enough."

"How old do I have to be?"

"Older than ten."

"How much older?"

"Go ask your mother, and close those windows. It's aired out enough in here."

Amelia left him to finish the paper and found Mom in the kitchen. "I wish he would quit," she said.

"So do I, sweetie, but he's never going to if you

keep badgering him about it like that."

"It's disgusting, Mom."

"Did you open the windows and pull up the screens? The air moves better when they're up."

"It doesn't matter. It's already everywhere. I can smell it in my bedroom."

"Close your door."

"Mom, the smell is already there."

"Close your door and open the windows."

"It comes under the door."

"Put a towel across it."

"Mom, I don't understand why we have to do all these things when all he has to do is stop."

Ralph Gardiner wasn't hard of hearing. He poked his head in the kitchen doorway. "I'm going outside to smoke. Then I'm going to bed."

Amelia followed him out onto the deck. "Don't you want a coat, Grandpa Ralph?"

"No."

"I can get your fleece. It's just inside, on the nail."

"No, thank you."

"Are you sure?"

The inlet sky was meant for stargazing that night but not for seventy-five-year-olds without a jacket. Grandpa Ralph lit up his favorite blend. The breeze caught his smoke ring and carried it out to sea.

"About the time you were born," he said, "your father and I were planning on enclosing this deck. Glass all around... Gas stove for nights like this... A nice, warm place to smoke in peace."

"Why didn't you?"

He shrugged. "Doesn't matter. We never got around to it."

Grandpa Ralph used to sit with her in his lap after dinner, and together, they'd read the newspaper, watch TV, or talk. Of course, he did most of the talking. He would blow smoke rings into the fireplace, and she would watch them float across the room like ships on the ocean. Once she was too big for his lap and knew what cargo the ships were carrying, her views on smoking changed. His wouldn't, no matter how hard she tried.

"Grandpa Ralph," she said, "I'm sorry I hurt your feelings. I won't bother you anymore. There's no point in saying the same things over and over or louder and louder. You know how I feel about it, and I guess I know how you do, too."

His pipe needed some attention. "If it'll make you happy, I won't smoke in the living room until the chimney's fixed. After that, all bets are off."

Amelia left him on the deck and went back to the kitchen, where Ruth was screaming about her and the favorite top she'd taken without asking. Ruth was taller than Mom. Other than having long, dark chocolate hair, no freckles, and nails that were either perfect or required stopping the presses to get them that way again, Ruth looked a lot like her.

"I just borrowed it, Ruth," Amelia said. "You weren't around. I said I was sorry." The top was over by the sink, soaking in a dishpan. It looked a lot greener than she remembered.

Ruth said, "You ruined it."

"I'm sorry, Ruthie. I'll pay you for it."

"With what? Mom said you only made a dollar."

"I have other money. I'll pay you whatever Mom says is fair, but I get to keep it."

Note from the Author

Granddad smoked a pipe and always smelled of it. Everything and everyone he came in contact with smelled of it. I never bugged him about it because everyone smoked back then, and I didn't know any better. Mom and Dad smoked cigarettes before the manufacturers finally admitted they were bad for you and everyone around you. Mom quit. Dad never did, but because one of us had asthma, he couldn't smoke in the house anymore. So, he did his smoking in the laundry room, which was off the kitchen and down a few steps. There was just enough space to fit the washer, dryer, and Dad. He'd open the back window and the door to the garage and sit on the steps reading the newspaper and smoking. He kept his cigarettes, matches, and ashtray on the ledge by the steps. I used to bug him about quitting, but he didn't want to, and I finally gave up. He knew how I felt about it, and saying the same things repeatedly wasn't going to change his mind. Oh, well. It's time for some weekday fun before Amelia gets to deliver to Amos again. See you then.

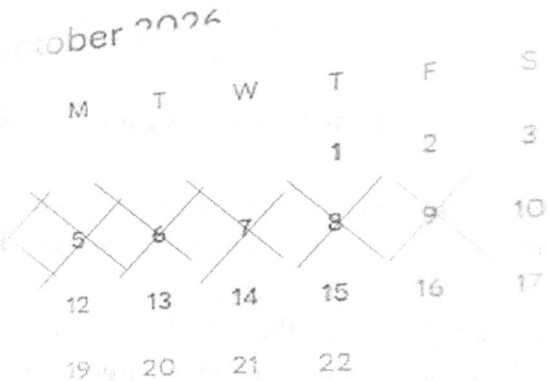

12) The Week Between

Mom walked up and down Cliffs Climb with Amelia after church the following day. It seemed safe enough to her in good weather. In bad weather, Amelia could either get a ride from Mr. Granger or find someone else to deliver there that day. She didn't want her taking the cutoff with all that traffic and no sidewalk, and under no circumstances was she to take Cliffs Climb in foul weather. After seeing Amos' cottage for herself and talking to Don about it, Mom didn't see any reason why Amelia shouldn't deliver there as long as she stayed on the porch and didn't bother the poor man. On the plus side, she was definitely doing that painting but needed to pick up more browns from the art store in Lambert first, and with the Milton Creek Bridge still out, that would have to wait.

Ruining Ruth's top had its pluses and minuses, too. On the minus side, Mom decided five dollars was fair, putting Amelia that much further away from a phone. On the plus side, she had a pretty top that fit and was almost green enough to match her Granger T. A few more washings together and, other than her five-dollar top actually fitting her and having "Delivery Person" stitched on it by Grandpa Ralph instead of "Delivery Boy" by Mrs. Granger, you could hardly tell them apart. When Amelia showed up for work that Tuesday wearing it, Mrs. Granger loved it before Don could say no, so she got to wear it. She returned the "Boy" T in case whoever replaced Jacks needed an L instead of an XL.

Amelia was the only one there that afternoon. The board was empty and stayed that way for two hours. She did all the homework she could without a computer her first hour and straightened up the area the second hour. Don gave her a quarter to drop his suit off at the cleaners on her way home, and she found a nickel and a dime on the sidewalk, making her profit for the day forty cents—infinitely better than nothing.

On Wednesday, Ricky was out back in the alley working on his scowl when she showed up.

"Nice shirt," he said.

"Thanks," Amelia replied. "Are there any stops on

the board yet?"

"There will be. Don might even give you one if you kiss his butt a little more."

"There weren't any yesterday."

"Only losers show up on Tuesdays."

"Why?"

"Because nobody orders on Tuesdays. It takes these morons till Wednesday to figure out what they forgot to pick up Saturday."

"Is everyone a moron, Ricky?"

"I'm not."

"I'm going inside."

"Good luck with that," he said, daring her to try.

She did, and he didn't stop her.

Don wasn't around when she came inside, and Little John was over by the delivery table studying.

"What are you working on?" she asked.

"Just math."

"Studying for the chapter test tomorrow? I saw you had one. I took it last summer. It wasn't that hard. Do you need any help?"

"I don't know," he said, snapping the book shut.

"Want to go 50-50 today?"

"No, that's alright."

"What's wrong, LJ?"

What was wrong was that he was sorry he hadn't told her about stealing from the mailbox, but he didn't think it mattered. He was even sorrier that he hadn't run back to tell her about the order mix-up right away. Maybe then, Don wouldn't have taken Amos from her.

"He didn't," said Amelia.

The next words out of his mouth were "But Ricky said," and that was as far as he got before Amelia stopped him. "It's fine," she said. "Don just said not to bother him again."

"He let you off?"

"I guess."

"Was it because your dad does business with him?"

"Privilege" was a word on one of Mom's vocab lists last year. It meant a right or immunity granted as a peculiar benefit, advantage, or favor. It meant that something wasn't fair, like her getting a second chance when he didn't.

"I'm sorry," she said. "Do you want me to ask Don if we can share Amos? It's no problem. Really."

"You'd do that?"

"Sure. Why not? I actually think Mom would be happier if I wasn't going there by myself."

"What about your phone?"

"I still want one, desperately, but I'm okay if it takes a little longer."

She asked Don. His answer began with no and ended with it wasn't up to him. They could partner on any other delivery, just not on Amos.

Their shift was from 3:00 p.m. to 5:00 p.m. Don put the first stop on the board after an hour or so of Ricky hanging out back throwing rocks at trashcans and her quizzing Little John on his math. It was a three-bagger for the Morons of Dumbass Lane that Don assigned to

Ricky. Another order came in right after that, a one-stop two-bagger. Don assigned that one to LJ but offered to add Amelia if they wanted.

The address was fifteen minutes away, and Little John could easily manage both bags without her, or Don wouldn't have assigned him to it by himself in the first place, so she said no thanks. If they couldn't split Amos, it wouldn't be fair to split any of them.

Don had to step out for a bit, and since Amelia asked, if anyone called, they were to let the answering machine take a message, and he'd get back to them.

"I can answer the phone," she replied. "I already did all my homework except the stuff I need a computer for."

He seemed hesitant despite her generous offer. Her hand went ring-ring, and she answered, "Hello, and thank you for calling Granger's Special Delivery. Would you like to place an order? We have some nice cantaloupes just in." She hung up. "See, Mr. Granger? I can be polite and courteous. I can even enter the orders and print them out for you."

"I didn't know they taught programming in the seventh grade," he said.

"It's just copying and pasting from one spreadsheet to another, putting in quantities, and pressing print. Toby showed me the template and how you did it yesterday. It's not very efficient, but it's pretty simple."

"Amelia, you're only ten. If someone comes in here and sees you working behind the desk, I could get in a lot of trouble. They have laws about that."

"Then, let me use your computer to do the rest of my homework. Answering the phone once or twice while you're out and writing down a few things isn't work. Besides, you're not paying me."

Don didn't know if not paying her was more or less egregious an offense than paying her vis-à-vis child labor laws, but he let her use his computer. If someone called and Toby didn't pick up, she was to let the machine take it, and if anyone mentioned anything about child labor laws, she was doing her homework.

No more orders came in that day, and even though Amelia took a different way home, she didn't find any change on the sidewalk or around the payphone at the Stop-N-Shop. That made her net profit for the two-hour shift a big fat zero. She didn't get any homework done on the computer either. Don had left it locked and wasn't the type to write his password down on a sticky note and tape it to the pullout tray or leave it in his desk drawer for someone like her or Ricky to find. She had to track down Mrs. Granger to get logged in, and after she had, Amelia found something far more interesting than homework—the CCTV program. Her curiosity had ten minutes alone with it: more than enough time for her to see that it was set to save the last thirty days of recordings but not enough for her to locate last Saturday's footage.

Note from the Author

Bravo, Don! You actually sprung for the complete CCTV package. I didn't think you had it in you, but whether or not you kept up the payments remains to be seen. The fact that the program was set to record and save the last thirty days doesn't mean it still is, especially if you're not paying for it. Oh, well. It doesn't matter. Jacks did it. Didn't he? Or... and this is where it gets a little fuzzy because it's so unbelievable... Was Ricky lying again when he told Amelia about Jacks? He lied about Petey getting fired and her losing Amos. Oh, Ricky, you brat—you didn't, did you? What if Jacks quit because he'd had enough. Maybe he found another job, like caddying at the Lambert Country Club, where he could make some real money. We may never know unless we press on.

13) It's Finally Saturday

Amelia endured three more nights of fish and two more boring days of schoolwork and homework, turning her science project/compost pile so Grandpa Ralph wouldn't complain that it looked like the village dump back there and doing chores around the house. When Saturday finally came, the sky was clear from horizon to horizon, and there were already six stops on the board when she got to Granger's. Ricky, who had three of them, including Tanner's, left her alone for once after a brief scowl acknowledging her existence.

Little John was a happy camper. He had two greens and was sure he'd aced his math test or at least come close. And she had Amos, all $73.51 of him, which at twenty percent was $14.70. Even rounded down, that was more than twice what she figured she needed each week to pay for a phone. However, everything had to be perfect for a twenty percent tip. In this case, that meant leaving the groceries on the chair, counting out the money and tip, getting next week's list, not disturbing the resident spider, ringing the doorbell, and leaving without bothering Amos.

The front door was wide open when she got to 10 Cliffside Terrace. Amos was sitting on a rocker at the far corner of the porch, facing the overgrowth of vines blocking his view of the inlet. She didn't say anything. He wouldn't have heard it anyway. She set his groceries on the chair, took $73.51 for Granger's and $14.70 for herself, snagged next week's bill, and rang the bell, but instead of leaving like she was supposed to, she took a peek inside the house, too quick of one to see much, but Amos was a terrible housekeeper. There were cobwebs everywhere. Mom would have a fit.

Amos stirred and got up. Amelia was still in the doorway when he spied her. "Can I help you?" he said.

"There are your groceries, sir," she said. "I didn't mean to bother you. I was just ringing the bell before I left."

"See anything interesting in there?"

How do you answer the bell if you can't hear it? Is there a light that flashes inside or something?"

He was too far away to read her lips. She tried one of the few signs she practiced on the way there.

He peered at it and said, "Sorry for what?"

She came a step closer. "Can you hear me now?"

"Of course not, I'm deaf."

"I made sure your order was okay this time, Mr. Evers. The fish looks great. It's my dad's. If you plan on freezing it, have some fresh first. There's a big difference."

"Thank you. I'll keep that in mind."

Amelia kept the grocery money in one pocket and her tip in the other, making it easier for her to take the tip out and offer it to him. "Does this count as bothering you?"

He waved the money off. "My fault entirely. I was just watching the sunrise."

It was a little after ten o'clock if Amelia had to guess, which she did, having no phone. Sunrise was at 7:01 a.m. that morning. She'd watched it with Mom on the deck, she with her hot cocoa, and Mom with her coffee. They'd just finished cleaning up after breakfast. Dad, Bobby, and Junior were somewhere far out to sea, trawling the sunrise catch. Mom sometimes fell asleep for a while, too.

"You could see it better without all the vines," she said.

"True enough," he replied.

"Why don't you have them taken out, Mr. Evers?"

"Why bother?"

"You'd see the sunrise better."

He nodded, "I can't argue with that."

"I can bring Mom's hand clippers next week and cut them back if you want. That'll help."

"I imagine it would. Good day," he said.

His labored step toward the groceries was her cue to leave. When she returned to the market, Ricky was out on his last stop, and Little John was reading a book. No more orders were posted, but Don was on the phone in his office, apparently taking one.

"What are you reading, LJ?" she asked.

"Nothing," he replied, "just something for English. You probably read it already."

"Do you want me to quiz you on it?"

"Nah, that's okay."

"I don't mind. I have to wait for Don anyway."

He said no thanks and returned to his book, the way Grandpa Ralph would pretend to be engrossed in the County Gazette when Amelia annoyed him.

"How'd you do on tips?" she said.

"Okay," he shrugged, not looking up.

"I made $14.70."

He said that was nice but was frowning.

Amelia said, "Is that more than what you got?"

"What do *you* think?"

"That I got more?"

"Yeah, you got more. Way more."

"That's not fair," she said. "I shouldn't get more for less work."

"That's just the way it is."

"We should pool our tips and split them evenly."

"We can't do that."

"Why not?"

"Ricky won't like it if we split Amos. He's mad enough already about you getting him."

"I meant him too and whoever replaces Jacks, to make it fair. Whoever is on that day should get an equal share of the deliveries, whatever they are. You shouldn't be punished for helping out the Grauls, and I shouldn't be rewarded for delivering to Amos."

"Sounds okay to me, A, but what do you think Don will say?"

Don was off the phone. He waved her in. "How was it?" he asked.

"Fine, sir. Here's the money and the list for next week."

He pocketed the money and looked the list over before locking it in his middle desk drawer. "And you didn't bother him, did you?"

"No, sir."

"Good."

She brought up the subject of tip sharing. Don was too busy to talk about it, so she left him to copy and paste items and prices from the master price list into the template, add quantities, and save it in the customer's folder, naming it by the date. Don had a folder for every customer who ordered and a spreadsheet for every order they made except for Amos. She'd looked.

Little John decided he could use some help after all, so they talked about the book he was reading until Don posted the order for LJ. He went by himself in case another order came in before Ricky returned.

Amelia was straightening up when he came storming in from the alley. She asked him how he'd made out. He answered with a scowl, went over to the board, and erased their latest game of Hangman in which she'd trounced him even though he threatened to give her an Indian burn if she did. He replaced the gallows with a skull and crossbones. "What do you care?" he said.

"Because. How much did you make?"

He ignored her, an improvement over calling her a moron.

"LJ made three dollars," she said.

"Good for him."

"I made $14.70."

Ricky spit on the skull, adding the final touches to his pièce de résistance. "What's your point?"

"It's not fair."

"I'll tell you what's not fair. That idiot Mrs. Tanner tipped me two dollars for a two hundred plus order."

"She's not an idiot, Ricky."

"You're an idiot."

"I'm not the one who got the two percent tip."

He threw the piece of chalk at her. "Are you saying I'm an idiot?"

"I'm saying we should pool our tips and split them evenly. That's the only way to make it fair for everyone."

"You think I'm stupid? I made twice as much as

Little John."

"So you made $6?"

"Yeah, I made six dollars. So what?"

"Your $6 plus his $3 plus my $14.70 is $23.70. Split three ways, that's $7.90 each. That's $1.90 more than you've got now and $4.90 more for LJ."

"And a lot less for you. That makes you an idiot."

"It's exactly $6.80 less, Ricky, and I'm okay with it because it's fair," she said. "LJ's in. I just have to ask Don. Do you want to or not? And just so you know, if he says yes, we're doing it with or without you."

"How do I know you didn't take more from Amos?"

She picked up the chalk and handed it back. "The same way I know you're not lying to me about only making six dollars."

Note from the Author

Civilization is based on relationships, and relationships are based on trust. How much we're willing to trust is based on how much trustworthiness has been shown. I'd put Ricky somewhere between "I wouldn't trust him as far as I could throw him" and "not in a million years," but Amelia wants to give him a chance to prove me wrong. I guess we'll see how that plays out next time.

HELLO
my name is

A

Granger's Special Delivery *Local 1*

14) A Brief History of Special Delivery Local 1

So, it was agreed. Amelia, LJ, and Ricky pooled their tips, and everyone went home $7.90 to the good that Saturday. Amelia said they should form a union and call themselves "Special Delivery Local 1" to make it official. Ricky said they were just splitting tips, not getting married. Little John didn't see why they needed a name or an official group. That left Amelia on her own when she approached upper management as the ranking and only member of Local 1 to tell Don they planned to pool their tips from then on in the interest of fairness. She presented their case, showed him the numbers, and explained the logic. Don said they could call themselves and do whatever they wanted. It was their money, but he didn't think pooling tips was a good idea.

The following Wednesday, fifty-six-year-old Frank showed up at the market wearing a Granger T. Don knew a guy who knew a guy who had a cousin who needed a second job. That was Frank. He lived north of Milton Creek and worked thirty-two hours weekly at the DIY Depot in Lambert. With Business 5 closed, it was a bus and a transfer to Granger's, and he hoped it was worth it because he needed the extra cash to pay for his medical insurance.

There were only three deliveries posted that afternoon. Ricky got the first, Amelia the next, and then Frank. At 5:00 p.m., when the shift ended and LJ hadn't gotten a turn, Amelia proposed a four-way split anyway. Frank objected. He barely made enough for the bus ride home and wasn't about to give a penny to a kid who hadn't done anything. Amelia asked for a show of hands in favor of discussing the relative value of work versus being on call for it and then putting the matter to a vote. Frank had a bus to catch. He took his two dollars, turned in his T, and quit. He needed a second job, not this. They voted without him to split the remaining take three ways. They were now officially Special Delivery Local 1, at least as far as taking a vote whenever they disagreed, not on the name or anything else about her stupid union.

That Saturday, Don sprung another new hire on them. Sean was fresh out of college and waiting for the right job to fall in his lap, preferably in his major, hopefully at least in a related field, but definitely not this. Don posted four stops. He got one — the Grauls. When Amelia explained that they split the tips so it didn't matter that the Grauls weren't paying, Sean was all in favor. He delivered his half-bag of groceries and returned at closing, missing two more orders that went to Ricky and Little John. It was time to divvy up, and Sean wanted his quarter slice of the $48.35 pie.

The uneven dividing of $48.35 by 4 wasn't the problem. Amelia said she'd do without the extra penny and round the others up. The problem was Sean took six hours to deliver one bag of groceries, and Ricky called him on it because part of that pie included his twenty dollars from Mrs. Tanner to make up for under-tipping him the other week. Sean, who it turned out majored in accounting, could have replied that technically, it's when the cash is received that income is counted for a business of his size. Instead, he said that Amelia told him it didn't matter. He'd get his share no matter what. His "what" had been spending the day on a library computer looking for a real job, not this shit. And now he'd like his money so he could be on his way, never to return. After using a few more words that would never appear on Amelia's vocabulary lists, Sean left with his one-quarter share, the only one not rounded up to $12.09. Amelia and Little John each gave Ricky four dollars of their own money, making his cut just north of twenty dollars. He wasn't happy about it but wasn't unhappy with them.

Delivering Amos' groceries happened in between the drama bookending that Saturday. It was blustery but not too chilly up on the cliffs. When Amelia got to the cottage, Amos wasn't on the porch, but it wasn't a nice day to stare at the hedges either. He'd left the rocker facing the inlet and placed a table beside it. She set the groceries on the chair by the door, took care of the bill, the list, and her tip, and went to work. Grandpa Ralph thought she should bring the lopping shears just in case, but she'd opted for Mom's hand clippers since they fit in her cargo pants pocket and required less explaining to Ricky. She cut a big enough opening in the vines with them for Amos to see the sunrise.

He was standing in the doorway when she came back to ring the bell and leave. "Thank you," he said.

"You're welcome, Mr. Evers."

"You've made it infinitely better."

Grandpa Ralph always said something is better than nothing, but infinitely better wasn't by much in this case. She said, "I should have brought the loppers. I can come back with them after church tomorrow and cut it back some more if you want." And as soon as the words "for five dollars" came out of her mouth, she knew she should have asked for more, just in case what looked like an hour's worth of work was more than she bargained for.

"Or maybe fifteen?" she said hopefully.

Amos said, "I'll leave the money. Take what you think is fair."

"What if I think what's fair is more than you?"

"Are you asking what the arbitration process might be to resolve a hypothetical disagreement?"

"I guess I'm worried I'll take too much or not enough."

"I trust you."

"What about LJ? Do you think you'll ever trust him again?"

Amos had no idea who she was talking about until she reminded him of his run-in with Little John at the mailbox not so long ago. He said, "When the boy admitted he'd stolen money and was putting it back, I directed him to Donald if he wished to make a full confession because I didn't care."

"Mr. Granger said it was up to you."

"Then, Donald is confused."

"So, is it alright with you if LJ delivers here? When the weather is bad, I need someone to sub for me, and Ricky's mom won't let him."

"I don't care who delivers."

"It would only be once in a while," she said, reassuring him that LJ would do as good a job as her.

Again, this time more emphatically, he said, "I don't care who delivers."

"You don't care if it's me?"

"Why should I, as long as the order is correct?"

It wasn't the first time Amelia had been reminded that she wasn't born as unique and wonderful as she was first led to believe growing up. She came into this world with a mixed bag of skills, just like everyone else. There were things she excelled at, such as everything related to school. There were things she was terrible at, like dusting, but only because she considered that a Sisyphean task and not worth the effort. And there were things she was no better at than anyone else, like delivering groceries. All she had to do was get it right. Beyond that, Amos didn't care. Theirs wasn't a friendship. It was a business relationship— Amelia's first—and she found it unsettling.

"Am I bothering you?" she said. "I thought I should check in case Mr. Granger asks."

"You may report back to Donald that all is well."

"Thank you, sir. Why do you call him Donald?"

"That's his name."

When Grandpa Ralph gave her an answer like that, she would say, "Pretend I'm not ten," and he would eventually tell her the real reason.

She said," Do you still want me to come back and trim?"

"As you wish."

A mail truck stopped in front of the house, and the mailman got out. Amos bid Amelia a good day, emptied the mailbox, and went inside.

Willy Demarest was a lifelong resident of Hook and a mailman for most of his adult life. Everyone in the village knew Willy, and he knew everyone, not so much by name as by their mail. He always said you could learn a lot about people by what ended up in their mailbox.

"What are you doing here, Highlights?" he said.

"Delivering groceries for Granger's," Amelia replied.

"Funny old coot. I see he took his money in. Did I ever tell you about when I found that wad of cash he keeps stashed in that box? You should have seen the look on his face when I knocked on his door to see if it was his."

"Did he say he didn't care?"

Note from the Author

Growing up, my brothers and I shared a paper route. I don't remember many names of the people on it, only how hard it was working every day to earn a tip when the cost of the newspaper was only sixty-seven cents a week. Seven papers, sixty-seven cents. All we had to do was put the paper in the door and only bother the customers once a week when we collected. When one of us was sick, the others would split their route that day. The customers didn't care. Except for the ones who lived right around us, most of them couldn't tell us apart. I don't remember how we first got the paper route, how many years we had it, or why we gave it up. I doubt our customers would either. We were just the kids who didn't throw their paper in the bushes for a few years. I'll see you next time for Amelia's further adventures in yard work and life lessons.

15) Just a Trim

It rained that Sunday, so Amelia didn't go back to the cottage after church, and it rained the following Saturday, not that hard, but hard enough that Mom wouldn't let her take Cliffs Climb. As Local 1's duly appointed spokesperson, she first approached Mrs. Granger to see if Little John could make the delivery. Shopping around for a better answer wasn't a usual tactic for Amelia because it rarely worked with Mom and Dad, but it had gotten her permission to wear a top that wasn't a tent. Unfortunately, there must have been an upper management meeting about end runs around the boss because Mrs. Granger said she'd have to ask Don, whose response was that if her mother wouldn't let her go, his hands were tied.

"But it's not raining that hard," she replied.

"I know, Amelia."

"And you know how busy it is on Saturday. Maybe you could convince her it's safe if LJ goes with me."

"I told you Amos doesn't want Little John delivering there."

"I'll deliver. He can wait for me on the path."

"No, Amelia."

"He technically wouldn't be delivering."

"I said no, Amelia."

The negotiations had reached an impasse. Amelia had tried Mom's way, but discussing it rationally wasn't working. It was time to act her age. She said, "You said it wasn't up to you, Mr. Granger, but Amos told me he didn't care if LJ delivered to him."

Don hadn't been called out by a ten-year-old since his son Toby turned eleven, but he still had the knack for deflecting from an inconsistency to an accusation. "Why were you talking to him?" he said. "I told you not to bother him."

"Mr. Granger, he was on the porch when I got there. He started talking to me first. What was I supposed to do? I couldn't ignore him, could I? Besides, I asked, and he said I wasn't bothering him."

"Why were you talking to him about Little John?"

"I don't know. It just came up. He said you were

confused about it."

Don closed the office door. "I'm not the one confused, Amelia. Sit down." She did, and he continued, "From now on, I don't want you talking to him."

"Even if he says something first?"

"If he does, you're to tell him you aren't supposed to talk to strangers."

"He's not a stranger. I deliver his groceries."

"And you won't talk to him again if you want to continue doing it. Is that clear?"

"Yes, sir. What about today?"

"Toby can handle it."

"Toby has a soccer game. What about Ricky?"

"Ricky can't."

"Why won't his mom let him?"

"You'll have to ask her that."

"You could call Sean or Frank."

"I don't think so."

In the end, Don called Mom and told her that the weather was clearing up and he was okay with Amelia delivering to Amos if she was. Mom said she was fine, too, as long as someone went with her. She suggested that one of the boys go along, and they split the tip. It only seemed fair.

As it happened, it stopped raining and turned into a lovely day long before Amelia and Little John ever got to Cliffs Climb, but she was happy for the company and someone to carry the lopping shears she'd brought to finish the trimming job at Amos'. When they arrived, she dropped off the groceries, took care of business, rang the bell, and ran back to the street, where she waited with Little John. That was as close as he was allowed under the agreement she'd negotiated on behalf of Local 1. She waved to Amos when he finally did emerge a while later. He squinted at them, emptied the mailbox, picked up his groceries, and went back inside.

When the coast was clear, she got to work. The trimming and cleanup would have gone faster with Little John's help. It took longer than she thought it would, and she made more of a mess to clean up than the fifteen dollars worth she planned on, but that was what she'd decided on taking before she started, so that was what she was going to take when she was done.

She was sweeping the clippings into a pile by hand when Amos opened the door and stepped onto the porch. He was a more imposing figure, standing erect and supporting himself with a garden rake instead of hunched over on his cane. "I found this," he said. "Use it or don't. Take it with you or leave it. I don't care. And don't forget your money. I left it in the box." When Amelia just nodded in reply, he said, "What's the matter? Cat got your tongue?"

"No, sir," she replied.

"Then what?"

"I'm not supposed to talk to strangers."

He found it amusing that she would call him that; at least, she judged as much from his cackle. He said, "Your name is Amelia, though you prefer to be called

A. Your father is a fisherman. His fish is excellent, by the way. You are competent as a delivery person and possess an unusual amount of intellectual curiosity for an almost eleven-year-old. Did I miss anything?" He steadied himself on the rake and held out his hand. "You may call me Amos. It's a pleasure to meet you, A." They shook hands to make it official. "There," he said. "We're no longer strangers."

"I thought you said you didn't care?"

"About what?"

"Me."

"I never said that."

"You said you didn't care who delivered your groceries."

"Indeed I don't."

"Oh," she said, realizing the two were different. "But Mr. Granger doesn't want me talking to you anymore."

"Donald said that?"

She nodded.

"Then, I suppose that's that," he said with a shrug. Setting the rake against the wall, Amos went for the groceries and promptly collapsed on the floor. Contrary to Local 1's labor agreement, Little John rushed onto the porch, and they helped him into the chair. She wanted to call 911, but none of them had a phone, so she asked Amos if he wanted her to run next door to the neighbor's back by the cutoff. Amos seemed disoriented for a moment but finally said no — it was just his knee acting up. He asked for the cane he had to leave in the kitchen because he'd needed two hands for the rake.

Mom had been crystal clear about not going inside a stranger's house, presenting a problem Amelia remedied with her own handshake. "It's nice to meet you, too, Amos, and it's okay to call me Amelia. 'A' never really caught on. This is LJ. He'll stay with you until I get back."

Amos turned toward Little John and thanked him. After he'd turned back toward Amelia, Little John said, "Are you sure that's a good idea, Amelia?"

She replied, "And just in case anyone still thinks we're strangers, your name is Amos. You're as old as Grandpa Ralph and don't get around so well. You like Dad's fish. I do, too, just not 71.43% of the time. You're deaf but not your whole life; otherwise, you wouldn't be able to speak. I know—I looked it up. You know how to sign, but you don't like to; you'd rather read lips." She shrugged in disappointment. "Which is really too bad because I've been practicing my signing so we wouldn't have to talk. That way, Don won't get mad at me. Also, I know you're a lot like me. You like to be alone, not all the time, just most of the time. Did I miss anything?"

She smiled, and the permanent wrinkles on Amos' face turned upward in reply.

Little John said, "Just hurry."

"Thanks," said Amelia. "I'll be right back."

Mom, Amelia, and Ruth (if she wasn't hiding somewhere) would clean the downstairs whenever company came over. Amelia's job was dusting (plus whatever Ruth managed to weasel out of). Amelia didn't like dusting, so she used the same method Grandpa Ralph used back when Grandma Jane made him do it. She dusted what she thought needed it and let Mom decide if it needed more. They didn't always see eye to eye on that but would have agreed that Amos' hallway needed some work.

Cobwebs dangled from the overhead light and every corner of the empty room. Years of accumulated dust covered the places on the floor that hadn't been walked on in forever. She hadn't asked where the kitchen was but guessed it was through the archway to her right, the alternatives being up the stairs or through two closed doors, one of which was probably the garage. The room beyond the archway had a fireplace and a bay window facing the porch. It was clearly the living room, but it didn't look lived in. The only furniture was a chair by the window, perfect for mailbox watching. A few dusty packing boxes lay scattered about, some empty, some with odds and ends in them.

She decided that the room behind the living room was the dining room, though there was no dining room table under the chandelier. In fact, there was no furniture at all in the room, only dusty green shadows on the wall of what had once been there. Grandpa Ralph would have had something to say to whoever repainted the room white without moving the furniture.

A swinging door separated the dining room from the kitchen. What distinguished the kitchen from the rest of the house was that it looked clean, at least by Ruth's standards, though Mom would have made her go over everything again. The room was barely big enough for a table and chairs, a sink, a stove, a microwave on the counter, and a refrigerator beside the back door. The gas stove didn't work. The microwave did. Amos' groceries were piled on the table except for the fish he'd put in the fridge. Underneath the groceries was an official-looking letter. It was lying open, and she read it, not being a snoop but curious by nature. It was short and to the point. As executor of the estate of a man she had never heard of, Mr. What's His Name, Esq. was simply providing legal notification to Amos that there was nothing for him in the decedent's will.

There was little else in the fridge and hardly anything in the cabinets or drawers. The only thing full was the wastebasket. Amos had one pot, one frying pan, one plate, one plastic knife, a fork, a spoon, one water glass, and one teacup. Done snooping around, she picked out a cane from one of several in the umbrella stand by the back door and returned to the porch.

When Amos said the cane wasn't the right one, she replied, "Yours is too short. You're bending over too much. Grandpa Ralph broke his toe once, and he didn't want to pay for a metal cane with an adjustable height, so he borrowed an old wooden one like yours from a friend. That one was too short, too, and Grandpa Ralph bent over so much his back started hurting. It didn't stop until his toe got better, and he didn't need the cane anymore."

Amos accepted the cane, thanked them both, and after telling Amelia to check the mailbox for her payment, went inside a bit more upright than before.

Note from the Author

I can see fifty reasons why things are about to get complicated. See you next time.

16) The Fifty

There was a fifty-dollar bill in Amos' mailbox; no roll of bills, no change jar, no note, just a piece of paper bearing the face of Ulysses S. Grant. If this were Mr. Peterman from next door handing her a fifty for helping him rake leaves, she would have thought he was joking, but not Amos. He wanted her to have fifty dollars when she only asked for fifteen. He wasn't letting her decide this time how much to take or what was fair; otherwise, he would have left the cash and the change jar in the box for her to take what she wanted.

Fifty dollars was enough to go to Mom to ask about opening a bank account to hold her growing pile of cash, the same account from which she planned to auto-pay her phone bill once she had enough saved. Fifty dollars put her months ahead of schedule. The problem was that it was too much money, so much that it seemed wrong to take. Little John suggested she put back thirty-five. She had $63.17 for Amos' bill in one pocket, her $12.63 tip, and a ten she carried for emergencies in the other. The only way she could put back $35 was to use $12.37 from the money that belonged to the store, and that would require some explaining to Don when she asked him to change the extra fifty.

She rang the bell, pounded on the door, and waited, then did the same thing twice before giving up and stuffing the fifty in her pocket. On the way back to the market, they talked about how nice a day it was. She quizzed him on the schoolwork she'd aced months ago. She asked about the classmates she'd never met in person and would probably be saying goodbye to remotely in a few months. They even talked about the weather, anything and everything but that fifty-dollar bill, until they got to the alley behind the store.

"What are you going to do?" he said.

"I can't keep it, LJ. It's wrong."

"You mean taking gifts from weird old men?"

"He's not weird."

"I wouldn't tell my parents if I were you."

"Why not?"

"He gave you a coat he said he didn't want. He gave you a rake. Who gives away their rake?"

"He said it wasn't his. It came with the house."

"Right. And now fifty dollars he won't take back, and that doesn't sound weird to you?"

She set the rake and loppers by the back door. "I donated the coat, and I'm giving the rake to Mr. Peterman. His is terrible."

"That's not the point, A."

Amelia took out the fifty, gazed upon the dead president's face, and sighed. Ulysses stared at her like Grandpa Ralph when he had nothing to say. She'd never owned a fifty before. She got to touch one once when Ruth was showing off, but never in her wildest dreams had she imagined having one of her own. Finally, she had something worthy of being framed and hung over the mantle between Dad and Grandpa Ralph's first dollars.

"I can't just throw it in the offering tomorrow," she said. "Everyone will see. I guess I could wrap it in a one and stuff it in the collection box in the back when no one is looking."

"What about your fifteen?" asked Little John.

"How am I going to break a fifty?"

"At the bank, like everyone else?"

"Mom and I go there every Friday to deposit Dad's checks. They know me."

"Wear a disguise."

"Don't be stupid."

"Buy something at the Stop-N-Shop."

"Like what, a pack of gum? Besides, they know me, too. Ruth worked there for fifteen minutes last year.

Everyone knows me, and eventually, Mom will find out, and she'll think it's…"

"Weird?" Little John said.

"I was going to say 'too much.'"

"Maybe Ricky can break it."

"No."

"Why not just say the fifty was your tip?" he suggested. "Count the $12.63 as money for the work you did. No one will ever know."

"I've never taken more than nineteen dollars as a tip. Ricky will know something's funny."

"He'll think you stole it, but that won't stop him from taking his cut and keeping his mouth shut."

"And that makes it right?"

He showed a little of his own exasperation in the face of hers. "I don't get why you think it's so wrong, Amelia. If we split fifty dollars three ways, it's fifteen dollars each. That's what you wanted for the trimming in the first place, wasn't it?"

"It's $16.66 and a penny more for the two of you due to rounding. It's *my* fifty. Don't I get to do whatever I want with it?"

"You're thinking of keeping it, aren't you?" he realized.

"I don't know. Maybe."

They went inside. Ricky was out on his third run, and they each had a stop on the board. Hers was the Grauls, and his stop was in the other direction, so they decided to split up. Don was in his office. He waved her in.

"What took you so long?" he said. "The Graul's order has been out there for an hour."

Amelia gave him the grocery money and Amos' list. "I'll get on it right away, Mr. Granger."

"How did the delivery go?"

"Fine, sir. I followed your instructions to the letter."

"Good." He tapped his pencil on the desk. "Amelia, I know you'd rather be outside playing with your friends on a day like this, but you made a commitment to work till three. You need to focus on that."

"Yes, sir. I'm sorry, sir. It won't happen again. I'll stay late if you want."

"No, that's all right. Just let this be a lesson to you."

West of Broad, past St. Peter's cemetery, and not too far either north or south of Main was the area of the village known colloquially as West Hook. The oldest houses in that part of the village bordered Main and most pre-dated World War I. The clusters of tract housing behind them just off Main came after World War II. The Grauls lived in one of those tracts, a nice one, on a quiet street. Their daughter, Heather, was jumping rope in the driveway when Amelia arrived. She was taller than Amelia and skinnier, had braces, and didn't talk much. She was a year older and a grade behind, which always seemed awkward whenever they were together at church.

"Hi, Heather," said Amelia. "I have your groceries."

"Seventy-eight, seventy-nine, darn," she said when she lost concentration and tripped up. "Now, look what you made me do."

"Sorry," said Amelia, offering her the bag. "Can I give these to you?"

Heather looked at the bag. "I'm supposed to be raking leaves," she said, though she had only gotten as far as getting out a rake and jumping rope till seventy-nine.

"Oh, okay," said Amelia. "By the way, I read that it's best not to rake in the fall. It's where the bugs winter over."

"I don't like bugs."

"We couldn't exist without them."

"If you're so smart, why don't you tell my dad? He's the one making me rake."

"How are you guys doing anyway? I haven't seen you at church in a while."

"We're okay," Heather shrugged. She told Amelia to ring the bell for her mom and started over at one.

When Mrs. Graul answered the door, she reminded Heather that her father would be home soon. She invited Amelia in and asked her to bring the groceries into the kitchen because she'd left her purse there. She offered Amelia two dollars, saying she was sorry it wasn't more. Amelia's counteroffer was the fifty-dollar bill because they needed it more than she did.

The awkward moment ended when Mrs. Graul said she couldn't possibly accept it, and Amelia refused to take any tip. Mrs. Graul was gracious and embarrassed. Amelia was sorry she'd made things worse by offering her money and hoped she wouldn't mention this to her mother tomorrow at church because it would be so embarrassing. Ultimately, the fifty went back to the market with Amelia but not into that day's tip pool. It went home, then to church the following day, wrapped in a one-dollar bill.

Note from the Author

My dad had an important job with a construction company. He was the one who said how much prospective jobs would cost, so the company knew to ask the customer for the right amount to do it. Ask for too little, and the company will lose money. Ask for too much, and some other company will get the work. Their continued success depended on him being right. Dad worked there for a long time. He took me there once. I got to play with the same toys he did, drawing and measuring things on giant sheets of drafting paper. I remember his adding machine was so heavy I couldn't budge it.

Unfortunately, while playing, Dad wasn't estimating. The boss noticed, stopped in, handed me a dollar, and said, "Go to the store and get me a pack of gum. Keep the change." What he meant was, "Get lost." With gum only twenty cents a pack back then, eighty cents was a 400% tip—way too much, even for a greedy little kid like myself. It didn't seem right, but I don't remember dropping it in the collection basket next Sunday.

17) The Gardiners Go to Church

On Sunday mornings, Amelia walked to church with Grandpa Ralph, though never before with Ulysses S. Grant wrapped up in a one and hiding under a tissue in her pocket. Mom and Dad were already a block ahead when they got to the light at Main. It was just the four of them. Ralphy would have gone, but he was away at school, and Bobby, Junior, and Ruth stopped going to Mass when they were given the choice, which occurred at some undefined age that was always a little older than Amelia whenever she asked. The discussions about either going to Mass or not became more complicated as she grew older, but never because she wanted to quit. It was more that she was worried they'd go to Hell when they died, and she'd never see them again, even Ruth.

The air was crisp and smelled like autumn that Sunday. The leaves were crunchy underfoot, and it was sweater weather for everyone except Grandpa Ralph, who had his overcoat and wool cap on. It was a challenging walk to Saint Pete's for someone his age, but he made it every Sunday. If you asked him why, he'd tell you he was taking full advantage of his only chance to smoke without being badgered by his family.

"Grandpa Ralph?" said Amelia.

He'd been counting the times (this being the fourth) that she'd questioned him about one thing or another since leaving the house. "What?" he said.

"How old were you when you got your first fifty-dollar bill?"

He thought about it, stopping to tamp his pipe and relight it. "No idea, but I remember when fifty dollars was about what you'd get a week. People nowadays carry them around like they're nothing."

"Mr. Evers gave me one yesterday for some trimming I did."

Grandpa Ralph hadn't asked when she borrowed his lopping shears. He knew he'd find out eventually. "Good for you," he said. "Did you put my loppers back in the shed like I asked?"

"It wasn't worth fifty dollars, Grandpa Ralph. I didn't ask for fifty dollars. He just gave me fifty dollars."

"Good. Keep it. Did you put my loppers back?"

"Yes, sir, but I don't deserve it."

"Who says you don't? Did you sharpen them?"

"I will. Grandpa Ralph, isn't it wrong to get paid that much more than what you're worth?"

"You're not some CEO getting millions, Amelia." His pipe needed some tending again. "Not yet, anyway. Keeping that fifty that's been burning a hole in your pocket since we left the house isn't wrong in the eyes of the law. If you think it's a sin, you need to drop it in the basket like you were planning to do or have a word with Father Timmons after Mass."

There were three Masses at St. Peter's on Sundays. Six-thirty Mass was understandably the least popular, given Sunday was the only day most people in the village got to sleep in. The assistant, Father Jim, celebrated that one and the eleven o'clock service, which was the one with the highest attendance. The eight o'clock Mass in between was the only service in Latin, the only one celebrated by the pastor, Father Timmons, and the one Grandpa Ralph preferred, even though his grasp of Latin didn't extend far beyond *et cum spiritu tuo*. The eight o'clock was also the one most fishermen and their families attended.

The Gardiners took their places in the family pew near the back of the nave. The pew didn't have their name on it. It wasn't theirs by right. They just always sat there, and no one else ever did, outside of the once-in-a-blue-moon visitor or tourist who didn't know any better. The few other families scattered about the church that morning were sitting where they always sat, too, including the Grauls. Amelia and Heather exchanged tiny waves and smiles.

"Where's your father?" said Mom.

"He said he'd be right back," Amelia replied.

"He'd better hurry it up. The altar boy is lighting the candles."

The altar boy in question was Ricky Finnerty, who looked angelically cute in a cassock and surplice, though a little frustrated because he was having some difficulty with the taller candles. He scowled when he noticed Amelia watching him.

"I didn't know Ricky was an altar boy," she whispered to Mom.

Mom replied that Mrs. Finnerty had mentioned he was thinking of going to the seminary in Lambert after high school. "I think this is his first time serving the early Mass."

"Mom, they don't let the altar boys count the money in the collection basket, do they?"

"I don't know, sweetie. What is taking your father so long?"

"Maybe he had to defecate."

Mrs. Cassidy, whose place was two pews in front of them, shushed her.

"Amelia," said Mom. "I didn't put that word on your list for you to use in church."

"Sorry. I'll go get him."

Amelia excused herself past Grandpa Ralph, who was praying for some peace and quiet and went to fetch Dad. She found him in the vestibule in a heated discussion with Don that ended with Dad saying, "We'll see about that."

Dad was fifty-five-year-old Bernard J. Gardiner. He was shorter than Grandpa Ralph with similar features on different frames. Whereas Grandpa Ralph was thin and lanky, Dad was barrel-chested, solid, and muscular, and had an on-again, off-again beard that was currently somewhere between the two.

At the moment, he was redder in the face than she'd seen him in a while. When Amelia told him it was time for church, his terse reply was, "Thanks, Punkin. I'll be there in a minute. I just need to use the restroom."

"Call me later," Don said as Dad hurried off.

Amelia said, "Was that about me, Mr. Granger?"

"Of course not," Don replied. "You're doing a great job, Amelia, or am I supposed to call you A now?"

"No, that's okay. Amelia's fine. I have a question, though."

"You always do. Make it short. Looks like they're starting."

"Are you still looking for someone for the team?"

"Why?" he said, now interested. "Do you know someone?"

"Heather Graul. And they could use the money."

"Isn't she a little young?"

"She's older than me."

That convinced him. "Tell her to stop by the store. I'll talk to her."

Mom and Dad were whispering loud enough for Mrs. Cassidy to notice when Amelia returned to the pew. She asked them the same question she'd asked Don. Was this about her? She wasn't fishing for a different answer. She was hoping the answer was the same.

Dad looked down at the daughter, who was growing up too fast. "It's nothing he won't get over," he said.

Mass began *In Nomine Patris, et Filii, et Spiritus Sancti* and ended when Father Timmons said *Ite, missa est,* the response to which was a resounding *Deo gratias,* except for the one visitor who wasn't following along in their missal. They said *Amen.* After church, Amelia caught up with Heather in the parking lot.

"Hey," she said. "Are you interested in a job? We're looking for a fourth to fill out the crew."

Heather shrugged. Amelia told her how much fun they had hanging out, doing homework together, doing math puzzles and word games, and playing hangman on the Board when they weren't delivering. Heather didn't seem interested until Amelia told her how much money they made, and all she had to do was show up at the market Tuesday after school and get Don's okay. Heather left, saying she'd have to ask her mom.

Father Jim and Father Timmons always heard confessions between the eight and eleven o'clock Masses. Grandpa Ralph needed a private word with Father Timmons, so Amelia came back inside to wait for him. No one was in Father Jim's line, so she entered the penitent box and waited until he slid back the window, leaving only the screen between them.

"Bless me, Father, for I have sinned," she began, making the sign of the Cross, "but I'm not sure it's a sin, Father Jim. Oh, and it's been three weeks since my last Confession."

Amelia was seven at her first Confession. Father Jim wasn't a priest then. St. Pete's was his first parish, and he was still trying to remember everyone's name. Hers was one he knew. "Why don't you tell me about it, Amelia?" he said.

Before making her first Confession, Amelia checked to see if the priest could see her through the confessional screen. He couldn't, but in a small parish like St. Pete's, it's only a matter of time before the priest puts your voice to your face and your face to your name. Then, the only thing keeping the priest from telling Mom and Dad is their vow of silence.

"Father, is taking more than you deserve a sin?"

"If by 'taking' you mean stealing, then yes, it is."

"It wasn't stealing. It was for work I did, but it's too much."

"Accepting generosity isn't a sin."

"He gave me fifty dollars for fifteen dollars worth of yard work, Father. That's 233% more than he should have."

That surprised Father Jim, who didn't think anyone in the parish had that kind of money. "Did he ask you to do anything extra for it?"

"He's not a pervert, if that's what you mean, Father. He's just an old man. So, keeping the money isn't a sin?"

"It doesn't sound like it. Have you told your mother?"

"Not yet."

Grandpa Ralph's disagreement in the Confessional with Father Timmons spilled over into the empty church when they left in opposite directions.

Father Jim said, "I think I hear your grandfather. Your penance is three Our Fathers and three Hail Marys. Now, make a good Act of Contrition, and you can be on your way."

The Act of Contrition is how the penitent says they're sorry for their sins and that they detest them not just because of the punishment in Purgatory they've earned as a result of committing them but because sinning is an offense against the loving God who made them. The Act of Contrition also expresses a firm resolve not to do it again. One Act of Contrition later, Amelia caught up with Grandpa Ralph, heading down Main.

"Father Jim said it wasn't a sin," she said.

"Good."

"What about you?"

"Everything's fine."

"What were you and Father Timmons arguing about?"

"Nothing."

"Grandpa Ralph, why are we taking the long way

home?"

"I'm not going home."

"Why not?"

They reached the light at 5 and Main. Amelia turned right. Grandpa Ralph went left.

"I'll be at Tanner's," he said. "Tell your mother not to hold lunch."

It was never good when Grandpa Ralph called Mom "your mother."

"I'll let Mom and Dad know," she said.

"Your father will be with me."

And calling Dad "your father" was even worse.

Ultimately, the fifty-dollar bill didn't go in the collection box at St. Pete's. It ended up in the cigar box in Amelia's top drawer with the rest of her growing pile of cash.

Note from the Author

We don't know Grandpa Ralph's problem, but he took it with him when he left the confessional. We may never know, but that's okay. Amelia has issues of her own that will involve some long division. Bring a calculator.

18) Dividing by Four

Heather Graul was eleven and a year behind Amelia in school, which always made things awkward. At one point, they'd been in the same class, but Amelia attended remotely and was only there the first semester before moving on, so they never really connected. Once in a while, they'd run into each other at church and be obliged to acknowledge the other's existence. Outside of that, they barely said hello and goodbye until the last few days. She showed up at the market Tuesday after school, wearing what she'd worn Sunday at church.

"That's a pretty outfit," Amelia said.

"My mom made me," replied Heather to the contrary.

"She just wants you to make a good impression."

"She wants to make sure Mr. Granger remembers me from church. Wish me luck."

Heather was still in Don's office when Little John showed up. Tuesday wasn't one of his usual days, but he had homework to do and couldn't concentrate with his mom and dad fighting. When Heather rejoined them, she was carrying an ill-fitting Granger tee draped over her arm and wearing a Granger ball cap that flattened her hair.

"You got the job!" said Amelia. "Congratulations!"

Heather wasn't as enthusiastic. "The harder I work, the better I do. The better I do, the better they tip. He must have said that a hundred times."

Little John waved. "Hi, Heather. How's it going?"

"Hi," she said, holding the tee to her front, demonstrating what everyone already knew. "It's an XL, and he doesn't have anything smaller. Amelia, do I really have to?"

"There's one I tried to shrink," Amelia said. "It's more of an L now."

"Can't I get one like you?"

"Sure, if you have a top that you don't mind dying to match."

"I've never dyed anything."

"It's easy. Just wash it in hot water with the one Don gave you. I can ask Grandpa Ralph to stitch 'Delivery Person' on it if you want. He did mine, but show it to Mrs. Granger first so Don can't say no. What days did he give you?"

"Saturday."

"What about after school?"

"Tuesday is the only day I get out early enough to be here by three. I have band practice the other days, and I'm in the stupid class play. By the time I could get here, it would be almost five. Mr. Granger said not to bother."

Little John wanted to know if she took the bus. She did, and with the Milton Creek Bridge still out, it took them an hour and a half to get to her house, a little less if they dropped her off at the market.

"You should walk," he said. "That's what I do, and I can get here by three, easy."

Amelia was curious as to how he beat the school bus home.

He shrugged. "I take the bridge."

"It's closed," she said.

"Only to cars."

"That's not what the sign says. Isn't it dangerous?"

"I go that way all the time. My dad said I'd be stupid not to."

"Isn't it illegal?"

"Everyone does it, Amelia. You'd know that if you actually went to school." Before going somewhere quiet to do his homework, he told Heather to meet him at the bridge around 7:30 a.m. if she wanted to see how it was done and not to wear a dress.

Heather didn't officially start until Saturday but decided to stick around for Amelia's explanation of how things worked at Granger's Special Delivery.

Amelia told her everything she needed to know about Don, the Board, the colors, the stops, the delivery table, checking your order, and various other things like Special Delivery Local 1.

Heather stopped her right there. "I have to join a union?"

"There's no dues or meetings or anything like that," Amelia explained, "but we vote on things, and they send me to talk to Don whenever we need to."

Heather asked the same question they'd all asked as newbies. "Why do you keep calling him Don?"

Ricky wasn't there to direct her to his shirt and call her a moron, but he walked in shortly after Amelia explained that it was because Mrs. Granger had stitched it on his shirt instead of "manager," like he wanted.

Trouble wasn't in uniform. Ricky was dressed to be going out somewhere. After sizing Heather up, he led with, "I'm Ricky. Who are you?" After ascertaining her name, age, and whether or not she had a decent bike with side baskets, he said, "I've been here the longest. If you need anything, let me know." On his way out to look for Toby, he added that Tuesdays were for losers like Shorty.

After he'd left, Heather said, "They call you Shorty?"

"Just him, I guess. I asked him to stop calling me an idiot and a moron, and this is what he came up with instead. It's better than Fish Face. He only called me that once because of my freckles. I think he's still shopping around for the right insult."

"He's cute. He's not your boyfriend, is he?"

"I'm not allowed to have boyfriends, Heather. Mom says I'm not old enough. Grandpa Ralph said if a boy tries to kiss me, I'm supposed to throw up on him. He says it works better than just saying no."

They hung out talking until it was nearly quitting time when Don posted a stop for LJ and H. It was just a green, so it didn't need two of them, and she wasn't in uniform, but it was on her way home and would give her a chance to see how it was done. They went off together, and Amelia went home.

The next day after school, Amelia was the first one there. Heather appeared unexpectedly wearing tight jeans and a Granger T that fit and was stitched, "Delivery Girl." Her name was written in sparkles on the brim of her cap, and she'd done her hair in a more ball-cap-friendly ponytail.

"Wow!" Amelia said, "and so cute, and you shrunk it to fit perfectly and changed it to 'girl.'"

"It's my mom," said Heather. "She looked at the tag, found the same thing online in my size, and had it shipped overnight. She stitched it this morning. The glitter was my idea."

"I thought you had band practice on Wednesdays?"

"I do."

"Oh," said Amelia, knowing what that meant. "Does your mom know?"

"She wasn't home when I stopped at the house to change."

"Are you going to tell her?"

"No, and you can't either."

"Heather, I can't lie about it to her if she asks. It's a sin."

"Just a little one."

"It doesn't matter what size a sin is. You still have to go to Confession to have it forgiven."

"It's not like you'll go to Hell for it, Amelia."

"Is that how I'm supposed to decide whether or not to do something?"

"Why are you making this such a big deal?"

"Because it sounds dangerous."

"You're not going to tell her, are you?"

Amelia told her not to worry. She rarely saw her mom and never talked to her about anything anyway, so the chances of her spilling the beans were so low you'd have to carry it out to three places for it to be significant.

"But I was hoping you might come over sometime," said Heather.

Though that might increase the chances of her telling on Heather enough that she would only have to carry it to two places to express how unlikely it was, Amelia said, "Sure. We could do homework together some afternoon if you don't have band, the play, or work."

"I meant to hang out."

"I'd like that, Heather, but when? We're both so busy."

Heather had trouble understanding how a ten-year-old who didn't go to school and had no friends she knew of could be too busy, so Amelia explained. "Monday we clean, Tuesday and Wednesday I'm here, Thursday I shelve books at the library, and Friday is my day with Mom. Saturday is work, and Sunday is church."

Heather said, "What about after supper?"

"Supper can be anytime between five-thirty and nine," Amelia said. "Isn't it the same for you?"

Heather said it used to be, but not anymore. Having dinner at the same time every day with her mom and dad was one of the only good things to come out of what happened.

They were a full crew that Wednesday, and Wednesday did not disappoint. Don posted greens from three Wednesday regulars that went to Ricky. Little John and Heather were paired on a red and a green, and Amelia had a $23.45 bag of last-minute things Mrs. Peterman forgot to pick up for her husband's big dinner that night with some rotary friends.

When the shift was over, $15 was the take, and it was time to divvy it up four ways, but Ricky wasn't about to. He'd made eight dollars in tips doing his three stops, and fifteen divided by four was only $3.75. Thinking he was insinuating that it was her fault, they were dividing by four; Amelia pointed out that one-fourth was less than one-third by only a twelfth. The tips were $15. He was only getting $1.25 less. It wasn't that big a deal, and it was fair. His counterpoint was that she was a moron who had only kicked in a dollar and was getting back $3.75.

"He's my next-door neighbor, Ricky. He thinks giving me a dollar is being generous. This is why we're splitting evenly. You got the good stops tonight. I get Amos on Saturday. It all evens out and makes it fair."

"The only reason we split Saturdays is because Amos equals an entire Wednesday."

"Ricky, if you don't want to split with us on Wednesdays, it's not fair for us to split with you on Saturdays, is it?"

"Ask them," he said, still cute despite his adolescent smugness. "They're the ones getting the shaft."

"You're the one shafting them, I mean us, right now by not splitting."

"That's how tips are supposed to work, not some crazy old whacko who lets you take what you want, and you're too dumb to take enough. I vote we just split on Saturdays. What do you losers say?"

They voted on it. Amelia returned Little John the $1.66 he'd given her for Tuesday's split, took her dollar from Mr. Peterman, and went home.

Note from the Author

Splitting the tips sounded like such a great idea—easy and equal, as opposed to a complicated negotiation involving the mathematics of the situation, resulting in a questionable agreement to which Amelia now feels bound. Personally, I was hoping for better. Time to move on. The next time we see Amelia, it will be Saturday, not just any old Saturday. Boo!

19) Halloween

Saturday morning was overcast and chilly after a hard frost overnight. Grandpa Ralph got up, complaining of coming down with something, and went straight to the bathroom, making Dad and the boys late getting out of the house because he took so long. Mom left right after they did to visit a sick friend, leaving Amelia alone to come up with something to wear for Halloween.

Her past costume ideas always came from the generations of belongings stored in the attic, some so old even Grandpa Ralph couldn't remember where they came from. She'd trick-or-treated as an angel, a devil, a witch, a vampire, a princess, and a mummy. She even dressed up as a field medic one year after finding Great Grandpa Joseph's helmet, canteen, and mess kit in a footlocker. This year, she dressed up as a Granger's delivery person clown. Her inspiration was Bobby's varsity letter jacket from when he played second base for the South Lambert High Yellow Jackets. The sleeves were solid blue, the center was blue-and-gold striped, and it looked silly enough on her that she could say she was a clown. To complement the jacket, she donned a fake nose she found in an old dresser, glittered her cheeks to highlight her freckles, and used Ruth's hairdryer to give her hair that frizzy clownish look.

She got to the market early. Don was in his office at the computer.

"Hi, Mr. Granger," she said at his door. "Trick or treat!"

Don looked up from the spreadsheet he'd somehow bollixed up. It was Halloween. He remembered her saying that the other day. "Just don't scare the customers," he said.

"I'll try not to, sir."

She offered to help with whatever was wrong, figuring something had to be. He declined but realized when he pressed the store intercom to call for Toby that he'd spoken too soon. Toby was at the post office getting the mail. He said, "You said Toby taught you about spreadsheets, right?"

"He showed me how you do yours," she replied.

"Good. Then tell me, where did all my prices go? I hit something, and now they're gone."

"Quit without saving and start over."

"I'm halfway through the order."

"Did you try 'undo'?"

He hadn't, so he did, and it worked. He thanked her and shooed her out of his office so he could finish.

"I can enter the orders for you if you want," she said. "I got an A+ in Keyboarding, Word Processing, and Spreadsheet Skills."

"They teach that in seventh grade?"

"Fourth."

"I can't pay you, Amelia. You know that."

"It's not work, Mr. Granger. It's fun."

One "thanks, but no thanks" later, Amelia was waiting over by the board when Little John arrived, cleverly dressed as a delivery boy. When he first got up, he thought about wearing something else but never got around to it. Ricky showed up next with a fake mustache and red wax lips. When asked what he was, he wasn't anything. It just got him better tips.

"What are you supposed to be?" he said to Amelia.

"A clown."

"What for? It's not like anybody's going to see you."

"*You* did. What do you think?"

"You look dumb."

Heather showed up wearing only her uniform

because she was trick-or-treating later on and didn't want to ruin her angel costume. If anyone wanted to come along, they should be at her house at 7:30 p.m.

This wasn't Ricky's first Halloween at Granger's. He didn't know exactly how much better dressing up on Halloween made the tips, but he knew what not wearing a costume got you — nothing.

Little John and Heather agreed to some minor wardrobe alterations so they'd all get better tips, and Ricky would get a bigger cut. They rolled their jeans up and cuffed them below the knee. Heather rolled her sleeves up like Ricky's, exposing a cute tiny butterfly tattoo on her shoulder. Little John rolled his sleeves up, too, and she drew a skull and crossbones on one of his arms and an anchor on the other. There wasn't much they could do with the caps but turn them sideways and tilt them a bit. And every pirate wears an eye patch, but the ones in the Halloween section of Aisle 1 were two for five dollars and weren't black, so they decided squinting out of one eye and talking like a pirate was good enough.

Amelia was only a clown until she walked out the door with Amos' groceries. Then the nose came off, the hair got pushed back where it belonged, and a futile attempt was made to remove the glitter on her cheeks. She kept the jacket because it was just an ugly bumblebee jacket that kept her warm on the chilly walk to Amos'.

When she got there, an ambulance was parked outside the cottage. Two serious-looking medical types wearing masks were loading Amos into the back of it. He wasn't moving, and his eyes were closed, just like Grandma Jane the day the ambulance took her away. That day, Amelia had Mom to hold onto; this day, she could only hug a bag of groceries.

Amelia wasn't the only bystander, just the only one crying. The neighbor who'd been walking her dog in the dead end when she saw Amos lying on the porch was still there. She offered Amelia a tissue and her reassurances that he was still alive, or at least he was when she called 911. They were taking him to Lambert General, where they took Grandma Jane.

Amelia returned to the market with $83.32 in groceries for Don to get aggravated about and a zero tip instead of the $16.66 that Ricky expected his quarter share of. After she almost cried again, explaining why, Ricky told her to forget it, and Don sent her home with a quarter to drop off his dry cleaning on the way.

Mom wasn't around when she got home, and Grandpa Ralph was napping in the living room. She found Ruth out on the deck on the phone talking to her boyfriend.

"Is that Trevor?" Amelia interrupted.

"Go away, brat."

"Where's Mom?"

"Not here," Ruth replied, going back to her conversation.

"Do you know when she'll be back?"

"Ask Grandpa Ralph."

"Do you know how to drive Grandpa Ralph's

pickup?"

Ruth told Honey she'd call him back. "Amelia," she said, "what do you want?"

"Can you drive Grandpa Ralph's pickup?"

"No. It's a stick. What's wrong? Is he alright?"

"They took Amos to the hospital."

"Who?"

"Amos. I told you about him."

"What happened?"

"I don't know. I can show you how."

"To what?"

"Work the stick."

"Why?"

"So you can take me to the hospital to see him."

Unfortunately, that was the stupidest thing Ruth had ever heard, so Amelia walked back to Granger's, looking for Little John. When she found him, he was hanging out with Heather and happy to explain how exactly to get across the Milton Creek Bridge without getting arrested or killed. It was fifteen minutes up Business 5 to Tanner's, another fifteen to the bridge, and mere seconds to climb over the barrier and run like the bad word he'd used until she got around the bend and was out of sight of the bridge. From there, the hospital was just up 5. She'd been there once when she was seven and never wanted to go back again. She couldn't stand the smells, she didn't like the noise, and she hated that it was a place old people went to die.

When she got to the ER, the letter jacket and Granger uniform played to mixed reviews. The guard who let her in with two thumbs up lettered at Lambert High, too. The nurse at the desk thought Amelia looked a bit young for high school and seemed skeptical when told the jacket belonged to a boy named Bobby — Amelia looked far too young to be dating anyone. When Amelia claimed to be Amos' granddaughter and demanded to know if he was still alive, the nurse wanted to see some ID.

One of the few times Amelia had to physically report to Lambert Middle School was to be photographed for her student ID. She handed it over, and to corroborate the lie, she told another. She said Gardiner was Mom's married name and Evers her maiden name. The rest was true: They couldn't call Mom because she'd gone out to visit someone and didn't own a phone. Dad didn't either. There was no one else but her.

The nurse was convinced enough to give Amelia the kid's version of events before letting her go in to see him. Grandpa Amos was sick and needed to stay in the hospital for a while to get better. In the ensuing Q&A, Amelia determined that he had suffered a mild stroke. They were keeping him at least until Monday before shipping him off to rehab.

When Amelia finally got in to see him, he was sleeping despite the moaning coming from somewhere on the other side of the ER. The last time she saw Grandma Jane was in that ER before they moved her to the ICU, where she died. His bed was raised almost to a sitting position, just like hers was. She jiggled it. He stirred and opened his eyes.

"Hi," she said. Amos wasn't reading her lips, so she moved to where she thought he was staring. "Are you okay?"

His gaze now seemed to include an awareness of her. He shook his head after she asked him again.

"The doctor said you'll be fine, but you can't go home for a while." She took his hand. "Is there anyone you want me to tell?"

He looked away.

She waited until he looked back. "I told them you're my Grandpa Amos, so they'd let me in to see you."

His reaction was indecipherable, a word she'd learned last week.

"If you want me to come back and visit, you should tell them I'm your favorite granddaughter. If you don't, that's all right too. I'm just happy you're okay."

When Dr. Simms came in to check on Amos, she was surprised to see Amelia there. She'd interned at Amelia's pediatrician for a year, opting instead for a less stressful career in critical care.

"Hello, Mel," she said.

"Hi, Dr. Simms. It's Amelia now."

"I'm confused. I thought your grandpa was Ralph."

They stepped into the hall, and Amelia admitted she was no relation to Amos. She just delivered his groceries. "Is he going to be alright?" she said.

"We hope so," Dr. Simms replied. "Do you know of anyone we can contact? Admissions said he had no ID on him when they brought him in. All we have is his name and address."

"Not that I know of," Amelia replied. "Are you sure he's all right? He didn't look all right."

"He's stable. There's no immediate danger for now."

"What do you mean 'for now'?"

"This wasn't his first stroke."

"It wasn't?"

"The CT scan showed he had another one recently, a mild one, not like this."

"And you're afraid he'll have more, even worse ones?"

"He'll be fine, Amelia. Where's your mother?"

"Visiting someone."

"Do you want me to call her?"

"She doesn't have a phone."

"How are you getting home?"

Not done lying, Amelia told Dr. Sims her sister was picking her up.

Dr. Simms was called away, and Amelia went back to see Amos.

"Do you want me to come back?" she asked him.

He shook his head.

"Are you going to be okay?"

Again, he shook his head.

"Isn't there anything I can do?"

A nurse came in to tell Amelia it was time for her to go.

Amos closed his eyes and replied, "Feed the cat."

Note from the Author

I love Amelia's choice of costumes. I went trick-or-treating as a hobo when I was ten. That year, we went to the convent to see if we could fool the nuns. As the only cross-eyed kid with glasses in school, they ID'd me immediately. In retrospect, I should have gone as a pirate, Cyclops, or even worn one of Dad's shirts buttoned over my head and gone as the headless horseman.

I wasn't wearing a costume the last time I saw my granddad in the hospital. I don't remember anyone saying he was dying either, but he did, and I don't remember him telling me to feed the cat because he didn't have one. Maybe we'll find out what that's all about next time.

20) Halloween II

Having been shooed so unceremoniously from the ER, Amelia didn't get a chance to ask Amos about the cat he asked her to feed. She had no idea he even had a cat, not having encountered one the only time she was in his house. Amos never ordered cat food or litter, and his house didn't smell like a cat litter pan. It smelled old and musty. There was only one thing to do.

When Amelia was nine, she hiked the inlet from the lighthouse at Hook Point to the Northside Docks and did it taking the beach. She slogged through sand and climbed over rocks, all because she'd heard it was hard and wanted to see for herself just how hard. It turned out it was hard enough that she never wanted to do it again. Walking from the hospital to Amos' was a longer walk, uphill most of the way, and a lot harder.

When Amelia got to his house, she headed around to the back, looking in all the windows because if she were a cat, she would be lounging in one of them, catching the late afternoon sun. She found a petrified potted plant, a dinner plate, and a bowl on the backdoor stoop. The door was locked. A light was on in the kitchen, but no one was there. She knocked to make sure. She rinsed off the plate and filled the water bowl from the outside spigot. Having done everything she could for the moment, she turned to go and nearly tripped over a cat on the steps, a calico to be exact, complete with the facial claw marks and patches of missing hair that meant Amos didn't have a cat. He was feeding a stray.

She squatted down to get acquainted, and the cat bolted, not stopping until it reached the fence. "I'm sorry," she said. "I don't have food for you, and I can't get in the house, but I put water in your bowl. I'll come back when I can. I promise."

Everyone had gone home by the time she got back to the market. Don was in his office. He called her in.

"Feeling better?" he said.

She wasn't but said, "I guess."

"The boys have all gone home, Amelia. I don't have

anything for you."

"Okay."

"It's a shame about the old guy," Don said, "but I guess your mother will be happy you won't be delivering there anymore."

"He didn't die, Mr. Granger," she said. "He's in the hospital."

"Oh," he said, surprised after what Ricky had told him. "Well, it sounds like we won't be delivering there, at least for a while. Winter is coming early, and if I know Martha, she wouldn't want you going up there in the snow anyway."

"I still want to work," she said, which was okay with him because the four of them made a good crew —not like that guy who knew a guy who had a cousin named Frank or that college brat What's-his-name.

She reminded him that What's-his-name was Sean and asked if any of the food spoiled.

"Abigail thinks the fish is a little off," he replied, "but the rest can go back on the shelves."

She asked if she could have the fish. It wasn't for her. It was for a project she was working on.

"Suit yourself," he said. "I think Toby stuck it in the freezer until trash day so it wouldn't smell up the back room. Why don't you go home, Amelia? You've had a rough day."

Amelia took the fish and went home, feeling depressed and guilty. She got there in time to help Mom finish the straightening up Ruth was supposed to have done before supper. It gave them time to talk.

Mom's day had been difficult. The friend she visited was in hospice, a new word for Amelia that meant nothing could be done but keep the poor woman comfortable until she passed away. Amelia didn't have a one-word answer for how her day went. So, she began at the beginning, and when she got to the part where they took Amos away, she did something she'd been trying hard not to do all day. She cried, ending the tale of her terrible, awful day. Mom didn't ask, and Amelia wasn't volunteering what happened after that.

At supper, her suspiciously quiet behavior had Grandpa Ralph convinced she was coming down with the same thing that kept him in bed all day. She admitted to not feeling all that great, which Junior interpreted as meaning she hadn't made any money again; otherwise, she would be boring them with her latest projections on when she'd be getting her phone. Amelia told him she hadn't made a penny that day and didn't want to talk about it.

Ruth showed up at the table while the family was eating dessert and was allowed to finish her meal before Mom and Dad escorted her to the living room for a private chat. Shooed from their comfy chairs before finishing the daily crossword, Amelia and Grandpa Ralph went out on the deck where he could smoke in peace and she could finish the puzzle. He was done with it and done with them. There were too many words in them to look up, more and more that weren't in Grandma Jane's dictionary. Amelia liked looking things up, though she didn't feel like running upstairs to get her laptop just then.

It was dark out. The sky had cleared. The moon was full. Grandpa Ralph had just moved on from complaining about the puzzle to complaining about that son of his who had yet to fix the chimney when the doorbell rang. Amelia went inside and through the house to answer it, passing by the living room where, behind closed doors, Ruth was in full whataboutism mode, blaming her for having done things just as bad (if not worse) and never being grounded for any of them. Mom put "whataboutism" on her word list during the last election. The technique can be rhetorically persuasive, but in the end, to say someone else did the same or worse as you doesn't make you any less guilty. It makes you both guilty, and Ruth was simply pointing that out to Mom and Dad.

Heather and Little John were at the door. Heather's angel costume was cute, and he was still, more or less, a pirate.

"Hi," he said. "I mean, arr, matey, trick or treat."

"We missed you," said Heather.

Amelia said she was sorry she couldn't make it and came out onto the porch, pulling the door closed behind her, muting the soap opera playing out in the living room. The Gardeners didn't get many trick-or-treaters, but Mom always put plenty of Amelia's favorite candy bars in the bowl by the front door, just in case. Anything leftover was fair game—Grandpa Ralph's rules, not hers. There was enough in the bowl for one each, plus one for Grandpa Ralph, but Little

John and Heather weren't there for that. They wanted to know how she was doing.

Amelia told them what she'd seen, what she'd done, and what she knew, which wasn't much. She asked them not to tell anyone. She wanted Mom to hear it from her first, just not yet.

Little John handed her six dollars. "It's your share," he said. "It was Ricky's idea. He scored big at the Hudson's. Usually, the dad answers the door, and he gets a couple of dollars. Mrs. Hudson answered it today and gave him a twenty, which was more like it."

"Are you sure?" said Amelia. "That's better than Amos."

"We put it to a vote. It was unanimous."

"Thanks. Does Ricky want to run Local 1 from now on? He's better at it than me."

"Heather asked him the same thing. He told her that your union is stupid."

"I guess it *was* a bad idea," said Amelia, thanking them again. "Maybe I'll see you Tuesday. We can hang out and do homework or read together or something."

They left, and when they crossed the street, they were holding hands and laughing. Amelia went back inside. The living room door was open. Mom and Dad were whispering over by the fireplace. Ruth was either inside cleaning it out as punishment so Grandpa Ralph could smoke in the house again, or she had been sent to her room.

Note from the Author

My brother was three years younger than me, and we shared a room growing up. Funny, I don't remember having my own room for the three years before that, but I remember little about the first three years of my life besides what I see in old photographs. Growing up, having your own room must be a completely different experience. Ruth would know. We should ask her how she feels about not having it anymore.

21) Ruth

Ruth had a single for seven years until Amelia came along. That gave her a substantial head start accumulating belongings, all of which had to move to make way for the roommate she hadn't asked for in the room that wasn't big enough for the two of them. When it was just a crib and Amelia was sleeping sixteen hours a day, things were fine, discounting the usual baby smells and occasional crying in the middle of the night. When Amelia started walking at eleven months, things began to change. She followed Ruth around the house like a kitten underfoot, always wanting to play. She laughed, she cried, she smiled, she pouted, but she never said a word until age three, when the first word out of her mouth was "Ruthie," and the second was "no."

Their relationship went downhill from there and hit rock bottom the day the Gardiner Brothers Moving Company came and took away Amelia's crib and Ruth's queen-sized bed, replacing them with matching double beds from the attic. Amelia was a big girl and entitled to an equal share of Ruth's closet, equal time at her desk, and an easement through Ruth's part of the room since the door was on her side. Separating the two sides of the room was an imaginary line down its center. Grandpa Ralph measured it himself and marked it with a notch in the window and one on the closet door after he'd had enough of their squabbling over territorial rights.

After saying goodnight to Mom and Dad, Amelia went up to her room. Ruth was sobbing under the covers. Amelia went straight to the desk and logged into her laptop. "Thanks for not saying anything about Amos," she said. "I figured you hadn't when Dad wasn't mad at me."

Ruth muttered that it was no problem.

"Why didn't you, Ruthie? It sounded like you were telling him everything else."

The covers came off, and Ruth sat up. "I was pointing out things they already knew about and didn't ground you for. Just because you're the baby doesn't mean you shouldn't be treated like the rest of us."

"You mean, like how I shouldn't have to do your chores all the time?"

"That's different. How many times have you been grounded?"

"None, but I never go anywhere, so it wouldn't be much of a punishment. Take away my Internet, and I languish," she said, ending her soliloquy with a flourish Ruth did not appreciate. "It means to be or live in a state of depression or decreasing vitality, Ruth."

"I know what it means, dork."

"Do you think Dad should punish me more or you less to make it fair?"

"Both."

"I'll make a spreadsheet and keep track. That's the only way to know if we're being punished the same."

Ruth yawned. "Don't be stupid."

"The hard part will be ranking each punishment on a scale of 1 to 10. They have to be numbers, or I can't add them up and compare them to make sure it's fair."

"Amelia, would you please stop talking."

"I got you to quit crying, didn't I?"

Ruth groaned. "Good night, Amelia."

"Goodnight, Ruthie."

Ruth rolled over, continuing her sob-a-thon facing the wall. Amelia added the six dollars from her friends to her spreadsheet. For lack of a better reason, she'd named it Phone Day because it told her the date she was getting her phone. The formula Phone Day used to come up with that date was complicated. Ralphy set it up for her. All she had to do was enter the dates and amounts each time money went in or came out of the cigar box. When she was done, she looked over her calendar to see what was on it for tomorrow other than church and checked her email in case Miss Melucci had answered her question on diagramming a sentence.

The windows rattled. The inlet's changeable weather was changing again. Branches from the oak tree Bobby hadn't gotten around to trimming yet brushed against the house. Grandpa Ralph's wind-sock out back creaked as it turned northeastward. Amelia closed her laptop. "Ruthie, I could have told you that blaming me for things I've done wouldn't stop Dad from grounding you for what you did. He knows what a whataboutism is."

"Thanks. I'll keep that in mind next time I'm being oppressed."

"He looked really mad. What did you do?"

"You mean this time or all the others? He's keeping a list."

"Do you want to talk about it?"

"What's the point?"

Amelia added the six dollars to the cigar box, recounting her stash to ensure the total agreed with the spreadsheet, and knelt by her bed to say her prayers. Amelia always began with a quick introduction to make sure God knew who it was that was praying. Then she would list everything she was thankful for that day, followed by specific prayer requests, and finally, her litany of God blesses. Grandma Jane used to sit on the edge of the bed when Amelia said her prayers, and they would recite them together.

Ruth interrupted when Amelia got to her, and the God bless was more than usual "God bless Ruth." She said, "Amelia, you don't need to ask God to make me happy."

"I was going to be more specific, Ruthie, but you don't want to talk about it."

"I'll be fine in a month."

"That's how long Dad grounded you for?"

"That's when I'm leaving."

"Where are you going?"

"I don't know."

"When are you coming back?"

"Never. I hate it here."

Amelia had a few more "God blesses" before getting into bed. "It's because of me, isn't it?" she said. "I'm the annoying little brat you never wanted."

"It's not you, Amelia. It's everything."

"The everything I took half of?"

"That's not what I mean, and you know it."

"What *do* you mean?"

"I don't want to talk about it."

"Are you moving in with your boyfriend?"

"I said I don't want to talk about it."

"Do you want me to stop praying for you?"

"No, that's okay. Goodnight."

They listened to the rain for a while.

"Ruthie?" said Amelia.

"What now?"

"Do you pray?"

"Of course, I pray — every night, to myself."

"Why?"

"Because you're supposed to."

"But why?"

"Because Mom, Dad, Father Jim, your teachers, basically everyone on the planet who believes in God says you're supposed to."

"Did God say we're supposed to?"

"He put it in a commandment, Amelia."

"The commandment doesn't say pray. It says to keep the Lord's Day holy. I do that by going to church. Other than God-blesses and thank-yous, I pray when I want Him to have mercy and change His mind, in case the will to be done isn't what I want."

"Is that why you said, God bless Amos, and please don't let him die? That was weird, you know, even for you. He's just a customer."

"He's going to die, Ruthie. I just know it."

"He's in the hospital. He'll be fine."

"Grandma Jane was in the hospital, and she wasn't."

"Grandma Jane had cancer. Why do you care so much about a total stranger?"

"He's not a stranger, and it's because it's my fault. I kept bothering him when Don told me not to. He knew Amos was sick. That's why he was so weird about me not bothering him."

"Oh, come on. You don't bother a person into having a stroke, Amelia. People just have them."

"The doctor said his scan showed he had another one right before this one."

"Which wasn't your fault either."

"What if I told you I was bothering him then, too?"

"Amelia, you bother everyone."

"Ruthie, he collapsed on the porch right in front of me. None of this would have happened if I had just called 911."

"Why didn't you?"

"Because I'm stupid. He said not to. He blamed it on his knee, and I believed him."

"That doesn't mean it was a stroke. It doesn't even sound like one. It's not your fault, Amelia."

"Ruthie, if he dies, it's me who killed him. I'll go to Hell." Amelia began to cry, making that twice in one day she'd embarrassed herself, not a record, but close. At least this time, the blubbering, sobbing, and moaning were under the covers where they belonged.

Ruth got out of her annoyingly small double bed, crossed the invisible line separating "my" side from "yours," and sat on the bed beside the sister she had never asked for. "Amelia?"

"What?"

"This isn't your fault."

"Yes, it is. Ricky's right. I'm an idiot, a stupid, stupid idiot."

"You are not responsible for what happened."

"He wouldn't have had a second stroke, Ruth."

"You don't know that. Besides, only God knows whose fault things really are. Everyone else is just guessing."

"That's what Grandpa Ralph says."

"And he's right."

"But what if it *is* me? I don't want to be a murderer."

"Amelia, you're not a murderer. You would never, ever hurt anyone on purpose. It makes me vomit how nice you are sometimes."

"You mean to everyone else but you, don't you?"

"Amelia, this isn't your fault. You're just a stupid, ignorant brat, and I love you."

Amelia surfaced for the waiting hug. "Ruthie, why can't you stay?"

"I told you. I can't live here anymore."

"You can have your old room back. I'll move to the attic."

"Sure, where there's no heat in the winter, and it's a hundred degrees in the summer."

"I'll give up half my space in the closet. I don't really need it. I only keep it to annoy you."

"Shut up."

They laughed.

Amelia said, "You can have your desk back."

"What about you?"

"Once I get my phone, I won't need it. I'll work in the kitchen till then. Please don't go, Ruthie."

"I can't live under this dictatorship any longer."

"Will I still see you?"

"Of course, you will," Ruth said, which was precisely what Ralphy had said before going away to college, and he'd only been home once that semester so far and was already talking about staying there over Thanksgiving break with his friends. "Goodnight, Amelia."

Amelia said goodnight and rolled on her side to face the wall, and Ruth returned to her too-small bed. Amelia lay listening to the on-again, off-again wind and the rain drumming on the metal awning over the landing window. During the lulls in the weather, she could hear waves crashing against the shore and a ship blowing its horn as it passed the lighthouse. When Ruth began to snore, Amelia rolled her way. Ruth was a mouth breather and always snored when she slept on her back. It usually only took a few taps on the wall to disturb her enough so she would turn onto her side. Then, she was good for the night. That was when Amelia closed her eyes and fell asleep.

Note from the Author

I've scheduled confessions from some people who need to make them next time. See you then.

22) True Confessions

Saturday was Halloween, All Souls Day on the Roman Catholic calendar, a day to pray for the souls of the faithful departed still in Purgatory, making up for the things they did here that were bad enough to delay getting into Heaven but didn't merit Hell, just a bit more suffering. Praying that the souls of the faithful departed rest in peace is a request for a reduction in their sentences, a prayer Amelia said every night for Grandma Jane just in case because Grandpa Ralph said she was a wild thing in her younger days. The

following Sunday was All Saints Day—the day
Catholics give thanks to the souls who made it, like
Grandma Jane, despite what Grandpa Ralph said.

Amelia snuck downstairs at 4:30 a.m. to call the
hospital. The nurse wasn't allowed to tell her anything
because she wasn't on the emergency contact list. No
one, in fact, was on his list. Dr. Simms wasn't on that
day, and the doctor who was on duty was too busy to
come to the phone, so they transferred her call to
patient services, a phone that just kept ringing. That
left her moping around the house until it was time to
go to church, but it wasn't just her. Everyone seemed
down that morning, even Mom.

They were walking to church together because Dad
wanted to have a word alone with Grandpa Ralph
when Mom said, "What's wrong, sweetie? It's not like
you to mope like this."

"I'm not moping. If anyone's moping, it's you."

"I'm just tired. Is there something you'd like to talk
about?"

"Something I *don't* want to talk about."

"Is it something you *should* talk about? Or is that
what you're still trying to figure out?"

"Mom, Amos had a stroke."

After a hug to make sure Amelia was as okay as
she claimed to be, Mom called out to Dad to go on
without them. They'd see them in church. "That's so
sad," she said. "Was that the hospital you called
earlier?"

"I had to know how he was, Mom, but they

wouldn't tell me anything."

"You have to be someone they're allowed to tell."

"I know. I lied. I told them he was my granddad to get in to see him yesterday."

"You went to the hospital? Why didn't you say? Did Mrs. Granger take you?"

"I walked. I took the 5 Bridge even though it's closed. I left the village without your permission. I pretended to be Amos' granddaughter because he has no one, and I didn't tell you yesterday because I couldn't until I knew he would be okay. Now, I don't. They won't tell me. I'm really sorry."

Many more details of her misadventures that day spilled out with her tears before forgiveness and absolution came with Mom's hug. Yet to be determined was her penance for breaking so many rules in one day. "If you're going to punish me," she said. "Could you please ground me? Ruth thinks Dad's being unfair."

"I'll need to think about it and discuss it with your father, Amelia. Thank God, you're all right. Please don't ever do that again."

"Mom, I was visiting the sick. Doesn't that count?"

"Amelia…"

"I was feeding the hungry, or at least I tried."

"It was a cat. Amelia, I'm serious. You could have gotten hurt or worse."

"Mom, it was totally safe. All the kids do it."

"Which makes you all guilty of trespassing and breaking the law."

"You're right. I'm sorry, but I asked Ruth to take me, and she said no. Mom, I had to see him."

"Promise me you won't do anything like that again."

"You were out. I couldn't call. You don't have a phone."

"You should have waited."

"He could have died."

"You put yourself in danger, Amelia."

"It wasn't dangerous."

"Sweetie, deciding whether or not something is dangerous is still my job."

"Do I have to move out like Ruthie before it starts being mine?"

"Did she tell you she was moving out?"

Amelia nodded. "When she's eighteen. She's leaving on her birthday, Mom, and she's never coming back."

"Where is she going?"

"I don't know. I don't think she knows. She has a boyfriend. I looked him up in the yearbook. He's kind of cute. Maybe they'll elope."

"This isn't the first time she's said she was leaving, sweetie."

"But it's the first time she'll be old enough that you can't stop her."

"Amelia?"

"Yes, Mom?"

"Please, promise you won't do anything like that again."

"Okay. I promise. I'm sorry."

"Will you stop moping now?"

Amelia was still working on that. "What about Amos?"

"I'll see what I can do when we get home."

"Or now, if only you had a phone..."

"We have a phone. It's at the house. Come on. Let's go. I'll call the second we get back. We'll leave right after Communion."

"I have to go to Confession first."

"Okay. We'll leave right after that."

"Isn't this your Sunday for coffee hour?"

"That's right. It is. I forgot. I guess it'll have to be after that."

"If you had a phone, we wouldn't have to wait."

"Please stop, Amelia. Please?" Mom said, exasperated.

It wasn't like her to say please twice in a row like that unless she really meant it, and it looked like she did.

"Mom?" said Amelia. "Are you okay?"

She wasn't, but she didn't want to talk about it.

They caught up with Dad and Grandpa Ralph in the vestibule and made it to their pew for the prayers at the foot of the altar that started Mass. Amelia spent the next forty-five minutes praying and listening to Father Timmons chant in Latin, which Grandpa Ralph said was the only proper language to keep holy the Lord's Day—a dead language most churches dropped sixty years ago.

The next confession came from Heather after Mass. She was waiting in Father Jim's line in front of Amelia. Father Timmons had to leave right after the service, leaving him the only option for desperate sinners such as themselves and ninety-year-old Mrs. McGowan. When asked where she got the pretty bracelet she was wearing, Heather confessed Johnny had given it to her. They were officially together now. She hoped that was okay.

Heather didn't take long in the penitent's box and left smiling. Amelia went inside, closed the door, and knelt down. "I have a lot to talk about, Father," she said. "I made sure I was last in line."

"That's very thoughtful," Father Jim replied. "Start any time."

"Bless me, Father, for I have sinned, but I'm not sure they're sins. It's been a week since my last Confession."

Father Jim reminded her that she'd said the same thing last time she was there. In truth, she had, but this time, it wasn't about her. This time, it was about a helpless old man who had nobody. She omitted the part about how it was her fault she hadn't run to a neighbor's to call 911 when he fell. Ruth was right. It wasn't her fault. She was just a stupid kid who didn't know any better.

She said, "Father, I don't understand how doing good can be a sin."

"Amelia, it's not the good you did. It's the sins you committed doing it. You were told never to leave the village without an adult, and you disobeyed. You lied repeatedly at the hospital. Those are both sins. To visit the sick is Christ-like. To get there the way you did isn't."

"But the result was good. Does the bad take all that away?"

"The end doesn't justify the means, Amelia."

"Does that mean the means justify the end?"

"Both must be justified in the eyes of God."

"But it was still good, wasn't it?"

"It was reckless."

"What was I supposed to do? I had to see him."

"When you're older, you'll understand there are other ways to accomplish the same good that don't involve breaking the Commandments."

She said she was sorry and asked if he would visit Amos at the hospital since visiting the sick was his job. He said he'd try to work it into his rounds.

Dad, Grandpa Ralph, and Don were in the vestibule in a heated discussion that Amelia wanted no part of, so she went outside to wait. Whatever had rattled and scratched at the windows the night before left behind a crisp November day, a nice day for one more confession, this one from Little John, who was on the steps outside, leaning on the railing, playing with his phone.

"Hey," he said.

"Hey yourself," said Amelia. "You got a phone."

"I've had it awhile. I just didn't have the money to add minutes to it."

"Paying by the minute is more expensive in the long run. Did you ask your parents about adding you to their plan?"

"They have a two-line plan and don't want to change."

"At least they have one. Mine don't even have phones. Are you coming on Tuesday? We can go through the math together so you can show them how much cheaper it would be to add a line. You can offer to pay the difference."

"That's okay."

"What about Wednesday?"

"No thanks, Amelia. I'm good."

It wasn't the first time Little John had glanced at the doors when someone came out. Amelia said, "If you're looking for Heather, I think she already left. Why don't you text her?"

"She doesn't have a phone."

"That's a pretty bracelet you gave her, LJ."

"I guess," he said, embarrassed.

"She said you two are a thing now."

"I guess," he shrugged.

There wasn't much else to talk about, and Little John wanted to catch up with Heather, so he took off and was halfway across the cemetery when Mom came out of the church crying. She'd just found out from Mrs. Finnerty that Phyllis, the friend she'd visited the day before, died last night in her sleep. Grandpa Ralph and Dad had business with Mr. Granger at the store, and they said it would take a bit, so Amelia and Mom started home.

On the way, Mom told Amelia how sad she was. Phyllis was older than her and used to live next door with her fisherman husband and two fisherman sons. Their families regularly had supper together, and she and Phyllis chatted nearly every morning after seeing their men off to sea until one day, her men didn't come back. She couldn't afford to stay in the house, so she sold it to the Peterman's and moved into an apartment upstate closer to her new job. At first, they kept in touch, speaking often on the phone and occasionally getting together in Lambert, but they inevitably drifted apart. Mom still had a family of fishermen to take care of. Phyllis had no one. "I'm so thankful I got to see her one last time," she said.

They didn't talk after that until they'd gotten home, when Mom said, "It's a nice day. How about we go for a drive?"

Note from the Author

When I was ten, Confession was something we were taken to involuntarily every Friday on the presumption we had done something wrong enough to confess to a priest. I remember times I didn't want to go because I had nothing specific to confess. I also remember being forced to confess something anyway. Sure, I wasn't perfect. Nobody but God is, but I wasn't the kind to keep track of my sins every week so I could recount them all for Father Harkins in the confessional. I knew I'd been bad, just not how many times. So, I made up numbers that sounded about right. I usually picked three for the number of times I disobeyed my parents. That seemed reasonable. I wasn't that bad a kid. As far as talking back to my teachers, if I didn't go with five times, I should have. My point is that God knew I was sorry for all the times, even if I couldn't remember them, even if it was more than three. That's it for confessions. Let's see how Amos is doing.

23) Hospital

When they got home, Mom said, "Pack something for lunch. We'll eat in the car."

Amelia made sandwiches from yesterday's leftover fish, wrapped them in waxed paper, and packed them in the thermal bag they often took on walks so long they might die of thirst, starvation, or both before returning to civilization. She packed a few carrot sticks and corn chips to balance the food groups, and the last two-pack of cream-filled chocolate cakes was dessert.

Traffic on the cutoff was light. "Can we stop at his house first?" Amelia asked, reminding Mom of the matter of the cat Amos had asked her to feed. She hadn't promised him she would, but she promised the cat, and it would be a shame to waste those leftover scraps she'd packed in the cooler under the sandwiches just in case the special person taking her to see him would say it was okay to stop.

When they got there, Amos' front door was wide open. After calling out, "Anybody there?" a few times with no response, Mom pulled it shut, but it wouldn't stay that way. The latch looked like it had broken long ago and wouldn't catch on the jamb plate without the deadbolt being engaged and the door locked, which could only be done from the outside with a key. Not having the key, their options were: Amelia could lock the deadbolt from the inside where no key was required and leave through the back door, or Mom could wedge the door closed with a page from a magazine she found on the back seat of the car and no one would have to go into the house with the door left unlocked and nobody home.

After securing the door, they went around the back, where Amelia filled the water bowl at the spigot near the backdoor and put the fish on the plate. A calico cat had been watching them from a safe distance, apparently disinterested. They spotted it when they first came around the house but had ignored it, hoping it wouldn't feel threatened.

"I came back," Amelia called, "like I promised."

The cat decided it was a good time for a preening. Amelia took a step toward it, and it bolted. As they were leaving, they saw it come back to the stoop to eat.

They got back in the car and kept going, leaving

them with only speculations and theories, though one thing was certain. The cat needed a name. Amelia wasn't going to spend the next half hour in the car with Mom, referring to the cat as "the cat." Their name was Calico until proven otherwise. Their gender was currently unknown, hence the gender-neutral pronouns. They had clearly adopted Amos because he never would have adopted them, and they liked Dad's fish.

"Why do you think he feeds Calico, Mom?" she asked.

"I don't know, sweetie. Maybe it's for the company."

"Why don't they just move in?"

"How do you know *they* haven't?"

"It didn't smell like it, and Amos puts the food outside. Can I keep feeding her?"

"What happened to the gender-neutral pronouns?"

"It sounds funny saying 'them.' It's like I'm talking about more than one cat. Can I?"

"That's a long way to go every day, sweetie."

"It's not that far. I can do it, Mom."

"Let's talk about it after we see how Amos is doing."

The detour took them west through a series of turns on two-lane roads, down from the cliffs to the one-lane Harper Mill Bridge that crossed Milton Creek a mile or so upstream of Business 5. They waited there in line with everyone else out for a Sunday drive through the local bottleneck before finally getting through.

"I want to stop at the mall afterward," Mom said. "I need more browns if I'm going to do that painting."

"Okay," said Amelia. "Are you hungry? I'm starving. Want half a sandwich?"

"I'm not really in the mood for fish."

"Me either. I'll split the carrot sticks with you."

Mom didn't want that either. She wanted a burger, fries, and a shake from that place in Lambert whose name escaped her. It was on Business 5, not far from the hospital. She and Phyllis used to stop there after matinees when they both had season tickets to the Lambert Community Playhouse. She couldn't remember the last play they saw there together.

Their turn at the bridge finally came, and it was smooth sailing from there down to Business 5 and past a 24-hour Stop-N-Shop where her burger-and-shake place used to be. It had twice the number of gas pumps as the one in Hook. They ate their packed lunches in the car in the hospital parking lot before going inside.

Amos was still in the Emergency Room. He had spent the night there because of what the nurse at the front desk called a paperwork problem. He had no wallet on him when they brought him in, no ID, and no proof of insurance. He either couldn't recall his Social Security number, date of birth, or where he was born, or he wasn't saying. They only knew his name and address. They were hoping either his daughter, who never showed up yesterday, or his granddaughter, who left without saying anything, could fill in the blanks so they could move him to a room and schedule him for rehab.

Saturday had been a day of questionable decisions made under extenuating circumstances. Amelia confessed them to Father Jim, and as far as God was concerned, she was forgiven with a little extra Purgatory time to wipe off that last bit of stain from her soul before letting her into Heaven. She confessed them to Mom with similar unspecified future punishment once Mom told Dad, but she hadn't made it right yet with the people she lied to at the hospital. She hadn't told them that the lie was all she could think of to get them to let her see Amos one last time before he died. So, she confessed that she wasn't who she said she was, Mom wasn't his daughter, and they didn't know anything about Amos except he had his groceries delivered once a week, fed a stray cat, and liked Dad's fish.

The nurse understood what it must have been like to see Amos taken away like that. She also understood what Amos must mean to them both to come all that way to see him when he wasn't family. So she hoped they understood just how hard it was for her to tell them that without ID, proof of insurance, or willingness to fill out any of the paperwork to accept financial responsibility, Amos was being discharged as an indigent patient. His condition was stable and not immediately life-threatening. The attending physician had already signed off on it. The hospital would bill him for what they'd done so far, but he wasn't getting any more on the house. Amos was free to go with them if he wanted. The orderly was on his way. If they weren't taking him home, the orderly would wheel him to the bus stop outside, where he would be abandoned with enough money for the 52 bus that stops there every hour on the hour, despite having no idea which direction to take it or where to get off.

The nurse's name was Sheila. Sheila was a good person with a difficult job. She'd been told a hundred times how terrible it was to turn the sick away, but never by a crying child giving them the hours for Confession at a church they'd passed on the way there. Sheila suggested they go in and talk to him. Maybe they could convince him. Perhaps it wasn't too late.

Amos was asleep and snoring lightly when they got there. He had the same wrinkly scowl as Grandpa Ralph when he slept, proving Grandma Jane was right that it eventually becomes permanent if you frown too much. After she died, Amelia used to sneak into Grandpa Ralph's room at night to make sure he wasn't dying, too. If she heard him snoring when she cracked open the door, she would go back to bed, knowing he was okay. If he weren't snoring, she would tiptoe over to his bed to make sure he was still breathing.

"Is he going to die?" said Amelia.

"No, sweetie. The nurse said he's stable. They prescribed a blood thinner that should keep him from having another stroke. Of course, it's up to him to have it filled and find a doctor to do the periodic exams to renew it every so many months…"

"...And actually take the medicine," said Amelia. "He won't do it."

"Why not?"

"I don't think he cares... about anything."

"Of course, he does. He feeds Calico. He cares about you. He gave you a raincoat and a rake."

"He wants to die, Mom. Did Grandma Jane give up like that before she died?"

"Grandma Jane died of cancer."

"But did she want to?"

Only Mom, Dad, and Grandpa Ralph were there at the end. It wasn't something they talked about.

Mom said, "She knew it was her time, sweetie, but Grandma Jane didn't want to go. She wanted to stay and see you grow up to become the wonderful person you are. I'm sure she's watching you from Heaven right now."

Amos stirred and opened his eyes.

"Hi," Amelia said. "Feeling better?"

"What?" he said.

His confused gaze traveled from her to Mom, who introduced then reintroduced herself to him after Amelia reminded her that he was deaf and read lips. How much he understood what Amelia said next was difficult to judge. He nodded at the correct times but struggled with his words.

"The hospital needs to see your insurance, Amos, or they're sending you home. If you tell me where your card is, I'll go get it and bring it back."

He stared at her as if peering through a fog.

Grandpa Ralph sometimes looked like that but always blamed it on his cataracts. "They said you need to go to rehab, but they won't let you without insurance." Her sense of urgency brought no reaction.

Mom led him through a series of simple "nod if it's yes, shake if it's no" questions, the result of which was that there was no one they could call, he had no wallet, ID, or proof of insurance, and he couldn't remember his birthday even after Amelia went through the months with him one by one. The only thing he said was, "Take me home."

A different nurse stopped in to get Amos dressed. When he was fully clothed and sitting on the bed, Mom asked to see the doctor who signed the discharge papers because Amos didn't seem at all stable to her. Maybe he could stand as long as he held onto something for dear life. Maybe he could hobble with a cane or walker if only he had one, but ask him if he knew where he was going, if he needed to use the toilet before they threw him out on the street, or even where the toilet was, and he was lost.

The attending physician had gone home, and the physician on duty agreed with her colleague. Amos was stable, so the hospital had no choice. That he could barely hold up his end of a conversation, let alone function independently, was something that hopefully would resolve itself, but there was nothing they could do but say they were sorry.

Note from the Author

When I was five, I borrowed my brother's wagon and took it for a spin. I flew down the sidewalk, over the curb, into and across the alley. Instead of flying over the other curb as planned, I crashed into it head-on, and Evel Knievel'd out into the street. The driver of the car saw me flying into him too late. His car was okay. The wagon didn't make it. I did, and I got my first trip to the hospital in an ambulance. I also got a broken leg that took three surgeries to fix and took forever in the hospital. I hated it. I attribute my nosocomephobia to that, a word Mom's likely to put on Amelia's next vocab list when they finally get home.

24) Going Home

When the Dodge died, Grandpa Ralph used to loan Mom his 1986 Chrysler LeBaron Town & Country Wagon. After Grandma Jane died and the State told him he shouldn't be driving anymore, he turned over the keys permanently. It had all the options Grandma Jane wanted, including power windows and a power bench front seat with an optional middle seat belt. As the only one short enough to sit in the middle without blocking the rearview mirror, Amelia always sat there whenever Grandma Jane was with them. When it was just her and Mom, she got the window seat.

Amos   sat   there,   belted   in,   confused   and

disoriented. Amelia reassured him they were taking him home. Mom said they had a quick stop at the Lambert Mall first to pick up her paints. When they arrived, she gave them explicit instructions to keep the doors locked and stay in the car. Nothing was said about staying in her seat, so Amelia slid into the driver's seat and pretended she was driving them somewhere far away. Where didn't matter, and maybe she wouldn't come back. See what Ruth said then.

"Who's Willis?" she said, bored of pretending to do something she'd already mastered in a video game. She had to get his attention and repeat the name she'd seen in the letter on his kitchen table. "Willis Jones. Who is he?"

"My son," Amos replied.

"Did he die?"

Amos nodded like Grandpa Ralph when she'd asked him if her goldfish was missing from the fishbowl because it had died and gone to goldfish heaven.

She said, "Grandma Jane died three years ago. I pray for her every night. I can pray for him, too, if you want."

She wanted to know why their last names differed and why the letter came from another country, but Amos was doing what Grandpa Ralph said grown men don't. When she leaned around in front of him to tell him it was okay to cry, he turned his head and looked out the window. When she tried to take his hand, he pulled away. When she tried to dab his cheek with a tissue, he recoiled like she'd blown her nose in it.

Purgatory is where most souls have to wait before going to Heaven. Grandpa Ralph compared it to Dr. Witherspoon's, where they never took you on time. Amelia's purgatory ended when Mom finally returned with the browns she needed, new brushes, and a stretched and prepped canvas. That all went into the wayback. The other package she'd come back with went to Amelia. It was a phone, not the one she wanted or the plan she hoped for. It was tiny, only 4G, and locked to a carrier she'd never heard of.

"Mom?" she said, not knowing what to say.

"It's not for you, sweetie. It's for me. The phone store was right there. They had one on sale with unlimited everything and no contract. I only had to pay for three months upfront. After that, it's month to month. They even set it up for me. That's what took so long. Sorry."

"You got a phone?"

"I've been thinking about what you said. I should carry one when I'm not in the house. I'm giving it a try. I can cancel anytime."

"They won't give you back your money."

"Yes, they will."

"Mom, it says right on the package it's non-refundable. They don't even want the phone back. That's how cheap it is."

To test exactly how cheap it was, Mom asked her to look up the number for County Social Services. Amelia wanted to know why when they were supposed to be taking Amos home. Mom replied that they needed help. Unfortunately, help didn't work on Sundays; only 911, and only for real emergencies, which they'd been told by the hospital theirs was not.

Amelia had inherited Grandpa Ralph's Boy Scout Handbook back when they were cleaning out some of his old things from the attic, and she'd read it cover to cover, the chapter on surviving in the wild many times. In it, she learned how to make a shelter out of whatever materials were in the area, putting together an eminently survivable one in the backyard that Dad made her take down because she'd used the wood he was saving for a project waiting for him to get around to for two years. She also learned how to start a fire without matches and why she should always carry a pack of waterproof ones in her pocket because it was nearly impossible to start a fire with just sticks and rocks. Most importantly, the Scout Handbook taught her that a person can survive three minutes without air, three days without water, and three weeks without food.

Air, in this case, was a given. As for the others, she said, "We need to make sure he has plenty of water. We can put a pitcher by his bed and a glass with a straw so he doesn't have to get up. And he'll need food. We should get him something at the Stop-N-Shop to tide him over. I'll go grocery shopping for him tomorrow. And I can feed Calico. I'll do it after school."

"Amelia, Amos needs help."

"We *are* helping."

"I know, but right now, he needs more help than we can give."

"Like what?"

"Sweetie, he should have gone somewhere to be cared for until he could care for himself."

"He doesn't want to." Amelia got his attention. "Say something. Tell her. Don't you want to go home?"

"Amelia," Mom said, pulling her back. "Don't."

"Mom, he understands what you're saying. He just wants to go home. He said so in the hospital."

"He shouldn't be left alone right now."

"But he wants to. It's his choice, isn't it?"

"Not in this case."

Previously, Amelia had considered eighteen the magical age at which she could decide things for herself. She'd never considered the possibility of that privilege ever being revoked. "I'll stay with him," she said.

"That's not a good idea."

"He's not a stranger anymore."

"I know that. It's not a good idea."

"Why, because I'm a minor? I can take care of him. I can cook. I can clean, and I can even do laundry. You know, all the things Ruth, for some reason, can't?"

"Don't be snide. How much do you weigh?"

"Fifty-five."

"Still? I thought you were putting some on. How much do you think Amos weighs?"

"I don't know. How much is Grandpa Ralph? They're about the same."

"He was 160 at his last physical. That's 2.9 times as much as you, rounded to one place, Amelia. You'd have to be an ant to pick him up if he falls, which he very well might."

"LJ can help. He did when Amos fell on the porch."

"That's a lot to ask of a friend, to come all that way every time he falls, especially after dark."

"He'd do it."

"Amelia, it's not just about falling, it's everything. He needs help with everything right now, and everything is just too much for us."

"We can do it, Mom."

Mom turned onto Cliffside Terrace and pulled up in front of the cottage. "I know you want to, sweetie, and I love you for that, but we just can't."

"So, we're not doing anything? We're just going to leave him? You said he'd die."

"I didn't say that. I said he can't be left alone. We're just picking up a few things."

"Where are we taking him?"

"Home."

"Home? Like our home?"

Note from the Author

Amos wants to go home, and they won't let him. When exactly does a person lose the right to choose? Good question, but one that won't be answered here. It's not in the Scout Handbook. Until next time…

25) Trouble at the Cottage

Grandpa Ralph would tell you that leaving your front door unlocked is asking for trouble. Trouble was already underway when they got to Amos' cottage. The friends Amelia had asked not to tell anyone about him being in the hospital came out onto the porch, laughing. When Heather and Little John spotted the car, they did what all kids their age do when caught in the act. They ran.

Mom told Amelia to wait there and got out. Amelia blew the horn and climbed out after her. Heather and

Little John, so quick to run away, stopped in their tracks and walked back to the car slowly enough to get their stories straight about just what they thought they were doing breaking into Amos' house like that.

Mom said hello to Heather and introduced herself to Little John, saying she recognized him from Amelia's description. Amelia wanted to know what they were doing in Amos' house. "Just looking around," was LJ's quick enough reply, but she was sure they were doing more, likely that thing she'd have to throw up on him for if he tried it with her.

Mom told Amelia to wait in the car with Amos while she went inside. Little John and Heather stayed on the porch, having taken Mom up on her offer of a ride back to the village and her word she wouldn't mention it to their parents if they never did it again.

Amos had fallen asleep on the ride there and, being deaf, hadn't heard the car horn. He awoke from someplace frightening and began struggling to get out of his seatbelt. Mom still wasn't back, and LJ and Heather weren't on the porch anymore. Amelia locked the doors and got his attention.

"You're okay," she said. "It was just a dream, Amos."

"Let me out."

"Mom said not to."

He said again, even louder, "Let me out."

"You'll die if we leave you."

Free of his seatbelt, the next obstacle was the door. He struggled mightily against the handle.

"Wait here," she said. "I'll get help."

She ran behind the house, expecting to find Little John and Heather getting an early start on what Ruth said she did with her boyfriend when she was their age. Instead, Heather was by herself because Johnny was inside helping Mrs. Gardiner with something. There was no time to chat about how cute he was, so Amelia returned to the front yard. A sullen Amos stared at her from his seat in the car. She waved to him and went inside.

The house felt and looked different. Someone had ripped apart the lacy valence of cobwebs over the living room doorway. The few boxes of books and odds and ends she'd seen in there before were tipped over, their contents on the floor. The dust on everything in the room was disturbed where it hadn't been before. This didn't look like anything Ruth would have done when she was Heather's age.

She heard Mom and Little John talking upstairs and found them in Amos' bedroom. The "something" Mom needed help with was the suitcase full of money she'd found in the closet when looking for something to carry his things in. Little John was helping her lug it back to the car. But the question was not what Amos was doing with a suitcase full of money in his closet. It was why Amelia was there and not watching him like she was supposed to.

"He doesn't want to go with us, Mom."

"Amelia, you know he can't stay here."

"What am I supposed to do?"

"Keep him in the car. We'll be there in a minute."

Amelia got back to the car too late. The door was open, and Amos was sitting on the sidewalk. He finally figured out the handle but had fallen, getting out, and now couldn't get up. "You were supposed to wait," she said, tugging on his outstretched hand. Mom was right. She didn't have the strength of an ant. "We have to wait for Mom and LJ. They'll be here in a minute."

They spent the minute sulking in each other's general direction.

"Please come with us," she finally said. "I know you don't want to live, but I don't want you to die."

Note from the Author

Our family moved twice when we were still together, once when I was too young to remember and once when I was around ten. I don't recall being consulted on the decision, but I vaguely remember our parents driving us by the place when it was just an empty lot, then a hole in the ground, and finally a house. It never occurred to me that the old house was no longer home until we drove away and Dad said we weren't coming back. I missed that old house for as long as it took Dad to drive us to the new one. That one wasn't next to the alley. It was next to acres of undeveloped woods and years of adventures growing up.

26) Home Away From Home

Amos was snoring when some kind soul finally let Mom make the left onto the Cutoff. There was room amid the clutter in the Chrysler's wayback for his suitcase full of cash and a reusable shopping bag with his essentials. There was plenty of room in the back seat for Heather, Little John, and the unoccupied middle seat between them. It was easier for Mom to see out the back that way. Amelia spent the time quizzing her about what she'd packed, then messaging Ruth the list of things she didn't think to look for or couldn't locate. That way, the annoying one could pick them up on her way home from wherever she'd disappeared.

Amelia pointed out yet another advantage of a

phone. Mom agreed, but they still couldn't afford one for her.

"But you got one," Amelia said. "It's an odious shade of green, has a terrible camera, and zero space to store anything, but it's a phone."

"Which one of us needs a phone, sweetie?"

"We both do."

"Then, let's assume we both do, but we can only afford to buy one now. Who should get it first?"

"But you don't even want one."

"I still don't, but you talked me into it."

Ruth messaged that she was still at the mall, wondering what Grandpa Ralph had done this time. When she heard she had to visit the men's department for Amos and not Grandpa Ralph, she was even less than enthusiastic but promised to pick up what he needed on her way home from studying with a friend, the one exemption to grounding she'd weaseled out of Dad.

A few catty texts back and forth, and Amelia put the phone away. Mom concentrated on traffic. Heather and Johnny were whispering sweet whatevers in the back, and Amos was snoring lightly.

Amelia wondered aloud what happened to the money in the mailbox. She looked over her shoulder at them, holding hands across the demilitarized zone. "The only thing in there was some mail. I checked." Neither seemed to have an opinion, so she gave them hers. She said, "He was expecting his groceries, so the money should have been in the mailbox when I got there. They found him on the porch, but there wasn't any broken glass or money lying around. That means he'd already put it in the mailbox, and someone took it. But nobody but us knew about the money. The only other person with a reason to look in there is Willy."

"You think the mailman did it?" Little John said, surprised.

"I don't know. I found the jar in the backyard near the swing. It was empty. I don't think Willy can throw that far. Besides, adults don't steal change. They leave that behind for a kid to take."

"Are you saying it was us?" asked Heather.

"I was thinking it was Ricky," said Amelia. "Was it you?"

"No," Heather said. "Of course not."

"We could take the jar to the police. They'll fingerprint it and find out who did it."

"No, don't do that."

"Why not? Don't you want to know? Or do you already?"

Heather already looked guilty as sin and admitted to peeking inside the mailbox when Johnny went inside. She found the jar; no roll of bills, just the jar and a spider that scared her half to death. She took the jar, emptied it of its contents, and dumped it in the backyard.

"It was only $1.53," she said. "It was no big deal, and you said he didn't care."

"It's still stealing," said Amelia.

"It's $1.53, Amelia."

Grandpa Ralph always said you can't argue the facts, but you can squabble all day long over what they mean. Amelia said, "Does that make it a venial or mortal sin? Where's the line? Is it a dollar amount, or do you think God takes other things into account, like whether you care or not?"

"Fine. I'm sorry," said Heather. "I'll give it back."

"Father Jim does Confessions after morning Mass if you can't wait till Sunday."

"I said I'd give it back."

"That doesn't undo the sin, Heather. Only God can fix that."

Mom decided she'd heard enough and turned on the radio, changing the station from wherever Amelia had left it after playing with all the knobs to the news. The upcoming election was the top story but not the only story. Work was scheduled to begin on the Milton Creek Bridge the next day and take two weeks. They were demolishing the old bridge Monday morning. That was great news for Hook but not so great for the kids losing their shortcut home from school. Taking the bus *to* school was okay. Taking it home was a total waste of the best part of the day unless you were Heather and could hold Johnny's hand all the way home. But Amelia saw another consequence. If Heather started taking the late bus home again and Little John waited for her, they'd get to Granger's too late to work weekdays, leaving just Amelia and Ricky to do all the weekday deliveries.

Amos began moaning in his sleep and listing hard

aport. Amelia intended to return him to an even keel, but with surprising, nascent ant-like strength, ended up tilting him the other way until his head rested against the window, a position Grandpa Ralph often found comfortable while giving Ruth driving lessons.

"Where do you think he got all that money?" she asked of no one in particular.

Mom had no guesses but said it was common for older people to keep cash in the house, though it seemed a bit out of the ordinary for it to be in the form of packs of bills kept in a suitcase in a bedroom closet. Amelia wondered if it were real because the alternative was a significant downward recalculation of her net worth after removing the counterfeit tips from her stash, resulting in a drastic change to Phone Day. Mom didn't know but said she would take a few hundreds and fifties to the bank the next day to have them checked. If the money was real, it could pay for a visiting nurse, a home healthcare worker, therapy, or anything else he needed — like a housekeeper — because he desperately needed one.

"What if he doesn't want any help?" said Amelia.

"You got him to come this far. Maybe you can get him to go just a little more."

Mom dropped Heather and Little John by the side of the road after they turned onto Brook Lane. They were off to take one last selfie at the old bridge before it was demolished. Everyone was doing it. Amelia could tag along if she wanted, but she couldn't, so they said they'd see each other Saturday at the store.

Amos awoke when Mom pulled into the driveway and hit that rut Dad had been meaning to fill in. He demanded to know where he was, who they were, and where they were taking him—all legitimate questions of kidnappers, which he realized soon after his outburst they were not. They were the ones taking him to Amelia's home. With their help, he made it as far as Grandma Jane's living room chair, where Amelia tucked him in with Grandma Jane's afghan.

Note from the Author

In 1998, Hurricane Mitch made landfall in Honduras, bringing heavy rains and causing catastrophic flooding in an area already prone to landslides. I was there for two weeks in 1999 with a group of volunteers helping to build a new village for people whose old ones had been washed away by Mitch. I'm not a skilled laborer, so I mainly helped by fetching things, holding things steady while the ones who knew what they were doing hammered them in place, and digging. A villager, another volunteer, and I were digging just outside the village one day when a woman carrying a basket on her head walked by. A man followed her, leading a donkey. Their child and everything Mitch hadn't taken from them was loaded onto the donkey. The villagers digging with us welcomed them to their new home. One of them called them lucky. His donkey hadn't made it. We have some homework to do next time. Till then…

pandemonium

extol

incite

catastrophic

normalize

broncophobic

destitute

retire

fortuitous

27) Vocabulary List

Nobody was home when they got there. On Mom's behalf, Amelia messaged Bobby, Junior, Ralphy, and Ruth, letting them know that Mom had finally gotten a phone of her very own. She asked if anyone knew where Dad and Grandpa Ralph were and if they planned to be home for dinner since it was already after three. Ralphy, still at school, sent his regrets on dinner and a thumbs-up on the phone despite Amelia's searing critique of its features or lack thereof. Bobby

messaged that he and Junior were at Tanner's and
would be staying to watch the second half of the game,
which they couldn't watch at home because Mom and
Dad had no subscription to stream it. In fact, they had
no subscriptions whatsoever and no cable T.V. The
Gardiners watched T.V. the old-fashioned way — in the
living room on Grandpa Ralph's old set hooked up to a
digital antenna that hung in the window or from the
mantle or from wherever he had Amelia move it for
better reception. Tanner's had cable, the drafts were a
dollar, and the fish sandwiches were half-off on game
day. As to Dad and Grandpa Ralph, they left at
halftime to meet Don at the docks and said they might
be late. No surprise, Ruth was ghosting her.

The leg of lamb had been in the slow cooker all
day, and the dining room table was set. The potatoes
were boiled and ready to mash. The corn chowder was
warming on the stove. The salad was tossed, and a
green veggie standing by in the microwave awaiting
irradiation. The only thing missing was everybody,
and the only thing left to do was wait until they got
home. Mom was over by the window, playing with her
new toy and keeping watch. Amelia was working on
the new vocab list Mom had produced seemingly out
of thin air while making dinner. Amos had been
napping in the living room until he needed to use the
bathroom. He was supposed to call for help but didn't,
opting instead to use Grandma Jane's cane to hobble to
the powder room. From there, he went to the kitchen
and sat quietly beside Amelia while she did her

homework.

Normalize," she said, reading from Grandma Jane's Webster's. "To make normal or average, to make something conform to or reduce something to a norm or standard. Okay, Amos. You go first." When he didn't go anywhere, she said, "You have to use it in a sentence that shows you really know what it means." He was reading her lips. He just wasn't responding. "Okay," she said. "I'll go first. Someone needs to normalize Ruth."

"Not funny, Amelia," said Mom, smiling as she glanced out the window, not because it was funny but because she'd triumphed over technology and figured out how to set up a group chat for the family. She messaged them for an updated E.T.A.

"But it's true," said Amelia. "The third definition in the dictionary is to bring or restore to a normal condition. Ruth is not normal. She needs to be normalized."

"She's a teenager."

"Has she answered a single one of your texts? Would you call that normal?"

"You said she was ghosting me. Isn't that normal? She's probably busy."

"She's not here, and she's grounded. Is that normal?"

"It was for Bobby when he was her age. You know why she's not here, Amelia."

"Because she hates it here."

"She doesn't hate it. She's growing up."

"Why are you defending her? The only thing normal about Ruth is that I had to do all her work again."

"*All* the work?"

"You know what I mean. Mom, we're like America and China. It would make life easier for everyone if we normalized our relations."

Mom nodded her approval of the sentence, "Better."

"Starting with her."

"I think you're being a little hard on your sister."

"That's because you've normalized her behavior, which is another sense of the word."

Mom decided that Amelia had a good enough grasp of that word and suggested she move on to the next.

"Okay," Amelia said. "The next one is brontophobia. Really Mom? Brontophobia?"

"It's a word, sweetie."

"So is disestablishmentarianism."

"Finish your homework, Amelia."

"Yes, ma'am. Okay, Amos. Want to guess what brontophobia means?" Amos didn't seem to want to do anything, so she said, "My guess is fear of long-necked dinosaurs." She held his gaze, not looking away even for a second, waiting for his reaction. A smile would have been nice; Mom was. A laugh would have been even better. Dad would have laughed. He liked corny dad jokes. Amelia would have settled for a flinch, a twitch, anything at all to show Amos was watching and listening from the Purgatory behind his blank expression.

"Thunder," he finally said.

"The abnormal fear of thunder," Amelia nodded, reading from the dictionary. "It comes from *brontē*, the Greek word for thunder. Brontosaurus literally means 'thunder lizard.'"

"Willis," he said, his gaze trailing off.

"Was he afraid of thunder?"

Amos began to cry.

We cry when we're sad. We cry when we're happy. We cry when it hurts. We cry when it stops. Sometimes, we cry and don't know the reason. Sometimes we just won't say. How long it lasts is uncertain, too. A crying jag can go on for hours despite Mom using every trick in the book, including bribery, but let Ruth make one snide remark, and the crying stops just like that. You never know. Sometimes, it only takes a little girl squeezing your hand and telling you it's okay, even though you know it's not, to make it stop.

"Destitute," she said, moving on to the next word. "Want to make a guess before I look it up?"

He didn't, by the look on his face.

"I'm sorry Willis died," she said. "You really miss him, don't you? I pray every night for Grandma Jane, but it's not the same as her being here." It was her turn to cry, and Mom's to say it was okay, and after a quick trip to the powder room, it was.

Back to the business at hand, she looked up

destitute. "The first definition is 'lacking something needed or desirable.' The example they give is a lake destitute of fish. The lake was destitute of fish, so they stocked it with chicken nuggets," she said straight-faced.

"There's a second meaning," said Mom.

"Mom, I used the first one. Doesn't that count?"

"Yes, but when was the last time you heard anyone say they were destitute of anything?"

"You just did."

Mom laughed. Amos stared. Amelia read definition two, "Lacking possessions and resources, especially suffering extreme poverty, a destitute old man."

She focused on him, and he on her, or he could have been looking right through her. She couldn't tell. "Amos, why do you live like you're destitute when you have all that money?"

"Don't be rude, Amelia," said Mom.

"Sorry, Mom. I was just using it in a sentence with the meaning you wanted."

"No, you weren't. Pick a different example next time. Mr. Evers hardly knows you."

To ensure Amos was no longer destitute of such knowledge, Amelia immediately launched into her curriculum vitae, beginning with her earliest memory: It was of her wearing her birthday cake and enjoying every minute of it. Next on the list was when she and Ruth made a cake for Mom's birthday. She was four. Ruth was eleven. The cake was a disaster that ended with them throwing it out and eating the icing from the bowl. She listed a few more food-related memories from years gone by before deciding she was starving and would likely expire before she could bring Amos up to date on her entire life. It didn't help that the lamb smelled amazing.

Mom agreed they'd waited long enough, so they ate in the kitchen. The lamb *was* amazing. So were the rolls she'd made, even though they'd been warming in the oven for over an hour. She'd put them in when Bobby messaged they were wrapping things up at the docks and couldn't exactly stop mid-bake when he told her fifteen minutes later that there had been a change of plans. Amos ate everything put before him, even the salad, which Amelia attributed to the dressing she'd made using Grandma Jane's secret recipe—the one Grandpa Ralph said Betty Crocker stole and put in her cookbook.

After dinner, they retired to the living room, which is how Amelia put it since "retire" was also on her list. Mom collapsed on the sofa with her latest read, a disappointing sequel to a book she'd really enjoyed. Amos got comfy in Grandma Jane's chair, and Amelia sat on the footstool beside him to finish her homework.

"Fortuitous," she said after looking the word up in the dictionary. "It means occurring by chance, fortunate or lucky. Its Latin root is the word for chance."

She looked at him. He looked at her. She said, "I wouldn't call it by chance that we met, Amos, but it's fortuitous that we did."

Amos put his head back and closed his eyes. When Amelia looked over at Mom, she'd already fallen asleep, leaving Amelia one word shy of finishing.

Note from the Author

When we were kids, our parents used to host card parties downstairs in the living room. I remember it being four couples at two card tables, playing bridge, switching partners every rubber. They ate, drank, snacked, and had a rousing good time. And by the time they all went home, Mom was too tired to do more than a cursory cleanup before bed. For some reason, she never got around to clearing away the leftover snacks. It was also strange how the bowls were always empty when she came downstairs for breakfast the following day. I blame it on the mice. The house was infested. One word left. See you then.

28) The Last Word

Amelia was a sound sleeper. Grandpa Ralph used to be a sound sleeper, but don't ask when he last slept through the night. When Mom looked in on her around noon the next day, she was still a lump under the covers right where Bobby left her after carrying her upstairs last night. Ruth's bed was empty. Mom sat down on it and was daydreaming when Amelia stirred.

"Time to get up, lazybones," she said.

Amelia looked at her, realized where she was, jumped out of bed, and ran downstairs. Amos wasn't in Grandma Jane's chair in the living room where she'd left him. He wasn't in the powder room either. He wasn't in the kitchen, on the deck, or anywhere else in the house. The car was parked in the driveway, and Grandpa Ralph's truck was still out by the shed.

Mom's explanation after she ran back upstairs began with her trip to the bank earlier, where they told her the money was indeed real. She came home and counted it. Grandpa Ralph recounted it. He came up with a thousand less than her, but the percentage difference compared to the total would require three decimal places to represent as a number. Amos had enough money in his suitcase to pay for the help they couldn't provide. All he had to do was want it.

"Where is he?" Amelia asked.

"At the rectory. Father Jim stopped by earlier to pick him up. He'll be taking him home once everything is ready."

"Is he better?"

"Better than he was, sweetie, but he still needs help."

"He doesn't want help, Mom."

"He does now."

"He does? What changed his mind?"

"I don't know, but he agreed to pay for a caregiver to stay with him until he can live on his own again. Our women's group will deliver their meals until the new stove comes, then the caregiver will take over.

Mrs. Graul is coordinating that. You and I are responsible for making the place livable before he gets there."

When Mom asked why she looked so sad, Amelia replied, "And when he gets better, he'll go back to being alone again."

"You don't want that, do you, sweetie?"

Amelia did not.

"I don't think he does either," Mom said, handing Amelia a rubber-banded roll of bills. The purple rubber band holding it together was a dead giveaway.

"Mom?" said Amelia. "I don't understand."

"It's the money from the mailbox."

Amelia's list of suspects included several people: Willy, Ricky, the woman who found him, and the EMTs, but never Mom. "Mom, I'm confused," she said.

"Amos wants you to have it."

"Mom, I'm confounded and perplexed."

"I can see that," Mom said with a raised eyebrow.

Amelia said, "I'm puzzled. How did he get it?"

"He can't remember. He found it in his coat. I guess he never put it in the mailbox."

Amelia counted it. It was enough for the phone she wanted, plus 2.5 years (rounded down) of monthly payments.

"Mom, I can't keep this. Can I?"

"He said you'll need it to get that phone you want if you're going to text with him."

"Now, I'm utterly confused. He doesn't have a phone."

Mom took out her odious green 4G throwaway with its terrible camera and zero space to store anything and said with self-satisfaction, "I found the one you want on sale and ordered it for him. It will be here tomorrow. I can have yours here then, too, if you want."

"I don't know what to say," said Amelia. "In fact, I'm totally befuddled."

And that was the last word on Amelia's list.

Note from the Author

Amelia wanted a phone. Amelia got a phone. That was the story, and this is the end, unless it's not, and we get to find out exactly how and where Amos got all that cash and why he keeps it in a suitcase. I wouldn't mind knowing that. Alas, poor Jacks never got a line. I still want to see the CCTV footage on that. I'm still not convinced it was him. And LJ and Heather? Will their relationship survive the seventh-grade dance? And aren't you dying to know which juvenile detention center Ricky winds up in? Personally, I think finding out what happened to Calico would be nice, too. There are so many things, and all I have to do is make them up and write them down, which, as of this moment, I haven't. Who knows where I'll be when you read this. I guess I'll either see you next time for further adventures or see you around.